Sudde

'I wouldn't ... ietly,
his own h... eep
inside her...

She'd seen ... treated all his
patients, no matter how young or old, and,
no matter how out of control he might get
in the throes of desire, she couldn't imagine
that he would ever resort to violence to get
what he wanted.

But if that was true… If Ben was a
trustworthy man…

'Who was it?' she whispered. 'If it wasn't
you, who was it?'

HEARTBEAT

LOVE WHEN *LIFE* IS ON THE *LINE*

In the intense atmosphere of the Emergency department, dedicated medical professionals race against time to save patients' lives.

But can these men and women also find fulfilment in their own lives – and in each other's arms?

Lives lived heartbeat to heartbeat...

This special collection of sixteen books from some of Medical Romance's most exciting, emotional and intense authors offers you a glimpse into the life, love, passion and caring of the Emergency department.

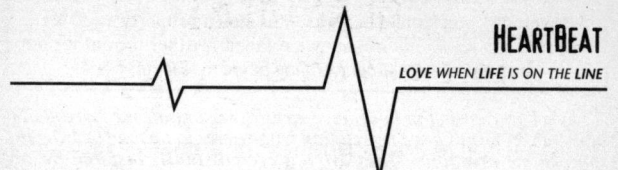

A TRUSTWORTHY MAN

Josie Metcalfe

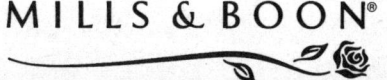

DID YOU PURCHASE THIS BOOK WITHOUT A COVER?
If you did, you should be aware it is **stolen property** as it was reported *unsold and destroyed* by a retailer. Neither the author nor the publisher has received any payment for this book.

All the characters in this book have no existence outside the imagination of the author, and have no relation whatsoever to anyone bearing the same name or names. They are not even distantly inspired by any individual known or unknown to the author, and all the incidents are pure invention.

All Rights Reserved including the right of reproduction in whole or in part in any form. This edition is published by arrangement with Harlequin Enterprises II B.V. The text of this publication or any part thereof may not be reproduced or transmitted in any form or by any means, electronic or mechanical, including photocopying, recording, storage in an information retrieval system, or otherwise, without the written permission of the publisher.

This book is sold subject to the condition that it shall not, by way of trade or otherwise, be lent, resold, hired out or otherwise circulated without the prior consent of the publisher in any form of binding or cover other than that in which it is published and without a similar condition including this condition being imposed on the subsequent purchaser.

MILLS & BOON and MILLS & BOON with the Rose Device are registered trademarks of the publisher.

*First published in Great Britain 1999. This edition 2004.
Harlequin Mills & Boon Limited,
Eton House, 18-24 Paradise Road, Richmond, Surrey, TW9 1SR*

© Josie Metcalfe 1999

ISBN 0 263 84496 X

142-0504

*Printed and bound in Spain
by Litografía Rosés S.A., Barcelona*

CHAPTER ONE

'IT'S starting,' Ben's companion whispered as the theatre lights went down and the overture began.

Ben welcomed the darkness, leaning back in his seat and folding his arms comfortably across his chest. At least in the privacy of a box he had room to stretch out his legs. His height could be a distinct disadvantage sometimes.

In his choice of companion, for example.

The music swirled around them, the voices rising and blending effortlessly to fill the whole auditorium as he glanced at her diminutive frame. He felt a smile touch the corners of his lips as he watched the enthusiastic way she leaned forward, intently following the action on the brightly lit stage. It was good to see that her usual down-to-earth pragmatism could be dispelled by her almost fanatical enthusiasm for opera.

He'd forgotten how long it had been since his parents had introduced him to her. She was a lovely girl, as well as highly intelligent, and she had let him know in her quiet, ladylike way that she was attracted to him, too.

She seemed to be everything he could want in a wife. Apart from the fact that his parents wholeheartedly approved of this daughter of their dear friends, the two of them had enough in common that they would probably have a very successful marriage, but…

But somehow she seemed so...delicate and insubstantial in comparison with Abby's inner strength...

Ben found himself glancing almost guiltily across at Carolyn again but she was oblivious of the fact that his attention had wandered from their special evening out together.

Unfortunately, it seemed to wander all too often in Abby's direction since he'd started work at St Augustine's and had met her for the first time.

Sister Abigail Walker.

Just thinking about her name conjured up an image of the woman he worked with in the accident and emergency department—her curvaceous, womanly body and her vivacious smile.

Her eyes fascinated him—lively, intelligent, sympathetic and full of laughter by turns. He'd been amused from the first by the perpetual battle she had with her exuberantly curly hair, the soft blonde spirals creating a halo around her head within an hour of being ruthlessly subdued into a tight knot.

He'd never seen that glorious mane set free but even when they'd been frantically busy, taking care of one of the constant stream of accident victims, he'd found himself imagining it often.

How long was her hair? Would it just reach her shoulders or would it cascade down to cover her nakedness in a riot of curls the colour of pale honey?

And her attraction wasn't just that she was pretty.

She had all the attributes that Carolyn had, and more. Unfortunately, if his recent information was correct there would be no point in asking her out because she also had a steady boyfriend.

Boyfriend! Ha! There ought to be a more appropriate word for an adult male companion. 'Boyfriend' made them sound as juvenile as teenagers, and there was nothing immature about Abby.

He remembered the incident a few days previously when she'd confronted a large, abusive visitor who'd been complaining about the service in the department as if it were a restaurant.

She wasn't a small woman. Judging by the height of her head against his own six feet plus, she must be five feet eight or even nine, but this man had completely dwarfed her. Not that it had made any difference to the way she'd treated him.

He felt a smile lifting the corners of his mouth as he remembered the calm way she'd led the man aside and explained the error of his ways. It hadn't been long before he'd been sitting quietly waiting his turn while other, more urgent cases were dealt with.

He'd also heard about the way she'd fought long and hard alongside Senior Sister Celia MacDonald for the extra staff they'd needed to provide the care their patients deserved. Having a couple of the more senior staff on maternity leave and his opposite number away on an exchange visit hadn't helped matters, but even with the help of part-timers they'd still been undermanned.

He wouldn't be at all surprised if it had been due to her sheer persistence that the extra funding had been found so that some of the pressure could be taken off the existing staff.

He remembered the fire in her clear blue eyes as she'd faced down the administrators at a recent departmental meeting, and an answering heat began to build deep inside him. He shifted in his seat, suddenly uncomfortable, and silently bemoaned the fact that it had become a common occurrence around the wretched woman. Now it was even happening when he thought about her.

It would have been all right if the spark he'd seen in her eyes had been directed at him. At one time he'd been egotistical enough to believe it had been. There had certainly been an instant attraction on his part.

At the time that he'd joined the staff there had been a sudden flurry of media interest because the accident and emergency department at St Augustine's Hospital had recently received national accolades for excellence. His appointment to the department had coincided with that interest and he'd found his photo accidentally featuring in more than one paper.

He'd quickly realised that while the A and E team were a pleasant bunch to work with there seemed to be a special awareness between himself and Abby Walker, her eyes seeming to hint at secrets only the two of them shared.

He'd silently resolved to make the effort to ask her out—to get to know her on a more personal level—but initially he'd just been too busy to do anything about it. His primary concern had to be the new job he was settling into.

Then, just a fortnight ago, he'd happened to overhear one of the senior paramedics bewailing the fact that he'd asked Abby out and had been gently but politely turned down.

'She's already going out with someone,' Ben had heard him say, and had been surprised at how much his own heart had sunk at the news. 'Wouldn't say who he was and she was really secretive about it. I bet you anything you like that it's someone on the staff.'

In spite of his disappointment, Ben had silently applauded her caution. There would be nothing worse than having to work closely with a colleague after a relationship had broken up, especially if everyone else in the department was watching your every move.

Even so, he would have liked it to have been himself who had put the extra spring in her step and the sparkle in her pretty blue eyes.

Was it possible to fall in love with a woman without ever going out on a date with her? The whole idea was positively juvenile but, then, that was exactly the way his hormones felt whenever he was around her.

He gave a resigned sigh when he realised that yet again his workaholic tendencies had served him badly. They'd emerged when he was still in school and had set his heart on a career in medicine. A chronic lack of any kind of social life had been the inevitable result then, and it looked as if the situation had just repeated itself.

His appointment at St Augustine's had been the fulfilment of a dream, and when he'd found himself unexpectedly bowled over by Abby he'd honestly been unable to believe his luck. Nothing like that had ever happened to him before.

If only he hadn't let work come before his urge to ask her out, perhaps...

No. He shook his head silently. He'd just have to grit his teeth and pretend he was adult enough to realise that some things were within his reach and some were not.

He fingered the small velvet box in his pocket and contemplated his resolve to ask eminently suitable Carolyn to marry him.

He was thirty-three already and his mother, especially, would be delighted to have him married because that would mean the prospect of the grandchildren she longed for was that much closer.

Unfortunately, he couldn't escape the uncomfortable feeling that he wouldn't be doing either Carolyn or himself any favours by going ahead with it, not when he wasn't going into it wholeheartedly.

A burst of applause shattered his introspection suddenly and he looked up to find the house lights had come up for the interval.

'Wasn't it wonderful?' Carolyn breathed ecstatically, her cheeks glowing with pleasure. 'I can't wait for the second half.'

'Shall we go and get a drink?' Ben offered, guilty that he'd been so preoccupied with his thoughts that he'd heard so little of the performance.

He rose and offered her his hand just as, with the briefest of taps, the door to the box was opened.

'Dr Taylor? Dr Benedict Taylor?' asked the man standing in the doorway, his eyes busily travelling from Carolyn to the dainty hand Ben had taken hold of and on to Ben himself.

'Yes. Can I help you?'

Ben instinctively noticed the man's air of authority. He might be nearly a head shorter than Ben but he was evidently accustomed to being in command.

'I'm Detective Constable Sharp.' He offered his warrant card as proof of his identity but Ben didn't bother to read the details. He was too busy wondering why on earth the police needed to track him down at the opera.

He'd made certain he wasn't on call tonight so that nothing could disturb his evening with Carolyn. Had there been some sort of disaster back at St Augustine's that required even off-duty staff to be called in? He knew that in the event of a major incident their excellent A and E department and intensive care unit always made them the first choice of destination for any casualties.

'If you don't mind, sir,' the man continued with a wary glance at Carolyn, 'the manager has made his office available. I need to have a word with you in private.'

'In private? Now?' Ben repeated, openly puzzled. What on earth was going on? If one of his parents had been taken ill, surely the man would have said so.

It was this reticence and the strange expression in the man's eyes that told Ben there was something seriously wrong, but for the life of him he had no idea what.

'Now?' Carolyn echoed in surprise, her hand tightening on his arm. 'But the performance is only halfway through and we had to wait weeks for the tickets. Can't it wait until the end?'

'And you are?' the officer prompted.

'Carolyn Messenger. I'm a friend of Dr Taylor's.'

'Well, I'm sorry, miss, but it won't be possible for Dr Taylor to stay,' he said quietly. Ben noted that his tone was perfectly respectful, but there was no softening in his eyes or his expression as he turned back to Ben. 'It *is* rather important, sir.'

'Will I be able to drop Miss Messenger home later?' Ben asked, bowing to the inevitable. 'I've never liked the idea of a woman travelling alone at night, even in a taxi. It isn't worth the risk.'

One dark eyebrow rose sharply but the officer didn't comment, merely signalling to someone outside the box.

'There is a car waiting and WPC Tait is available to take the young lady home,' he said quietly.

'Can't I go with him?' Carolyn asked, and Ben felt the trembling in her hands as she tightened them around his arm even as her chin lifted.

'Can you verify Dr Taylor's whereabouts over the last twenty-four hours?' DC Sharp asked.

'Well, not exactly,' Carolyn admitted, and Ben caught the quick glance she threw his way. He noticed that she didn't quite meet his gaze and her grip on his arm was loosening as though she was just beginning to realise what sort of situation she might have become embroiled in. 'I've been away at my sister's. She's just had a baby. I only came back up to town for the opera this evening because of the tickets.'

'In which case, it would be better if WPC Tait drove you home,' said DC Sharp firmly.

'But…' she began, but Ben could tell her heart wasn't in it.

'Don't worry, Carolyn,' he said quietly, giving her limp hands a pat before he drew his arm away. 'It'll be all right.'

'You'll let me know as soon as you get home?' she begged, her pale eyes wide with uncertainty as he helped her on with her coat.

'Of course,' he said, infusing all the reassurance he could muster into his voice, but the cold expression he saw in the policeman's eyes sent an apprehensive shiver up his spine.

As he watched her leave the box he registered the fact that she didn't look back at him, and he could see the way she was clutching her handbag in trembling hands as she disappeared from view.

'*Now* can you tell me what this is about?' Ben asked

as he planted his feet stubbornly and met the older man's gaze. 'Can I take it that nothing's happened to my parents and it isn't anything to do with the hospital?'

'That's correct, sir, but I really think it would be better if we had this conversation elsewhere,' DC Sharp said as a burst of laughter preceded a group of patrons going in search of a drink. They paused outside the open door to the box and peered inquisitively inside.

Realising that whatever this was about required more privacy than they would find here, Ben had to agree. As he followed DC Sharp into the corridor they were quickly surrounded by the throng.

As they made their way towards the manager's office Ben couldn't help contrasting their carefree air with the solid lump of dread sitting in the pit of his stomach.

Abby wrapped her arms around herself but still she couldn't stop shaking. She hadn't let herself cry yet—didn't dare or she knew she'd completely fall apart.

It had been hours now, but she was determined to keep herself under control until she'd done everything that had to be done. At the moment she was only being sustained by her anger. If she let herself dwell on her hurt and disappointment she didn't think she'd survive, not after all the rosy dreams she'd started to weave.

How could he have done it to her?

How could he have done it to *anyone*?

Apart from anything else, the whole thing just didn't make sense. It didn't fit with the man she'd come to know as they worked together at the hospital.

The corner of her mouth lifted in the beginnings of a smile when she remembered the elaborate secrecy they'd employed to prevent any of their colleagues from finding out about their relationship.

A part of her had been so certain of her unfolding feelings that she'd been ready to say damn to the gossips, but he'd advised caution—at least for a while.

The sharp sting of the split in her lip reminded her of the stinging slap that had caused it, and the dull throb of her cheek-bone drew attention to the bruising marring her ghastly pale skin.

She'd only caught a brief glimpse of herself in the mirror on the wall of the special suite she'd been taken to before she'd hastily turned her back on the image.

In spite of her instinctive longings, she'd known that it was important that the police surgeon collected his samples before she'd cleaned herself up. As soon as the indignities of the medical examination were over she'd stood under the shower for ages while she'd soaped herself over and over again. She still didn't feel clean.

Eventually it had been pity for the poor policewoman waiting for her to emerge that had forced her out again, knowing that the next ordeal she faced had been a detailed interview.

There were other bruises she'd discovered, apart from the ones visible on her face. She hadn't realised just how many until she'd given up her clothing as evidence and the police surgeon had begun to catalogue each abrasion and collect samples.

That had been hours ago now—heaven only knew exactly how long because time had ceased to have any real meaning for her.

It was partly her own fault that she was still here

because when the process had been explained to her, and she was told she'd have to return at a later time for the identity parade, she suddenly couldn't bear it any more.

Fighting hysteria, she'd begged them to see if they could do it straight away. She'd known it was important for the police to follow procedure but the thought of having that hanging overhead had been unbearable.

At least she was grateful that she'd finally got some warm clothes on.

She looked down at the slightly scruffy navy tracksuit that someone had fetched for her from her flat. In spite of the thick, fleecy fabric, it hardly seemed warm enough to ward off the chills that racked her even in the warmth of the room.

A sound drew her attention to the policewoman sitting quietly on the other side of the room.

Apparently Beth Cassidy was a specially trained liaison officer and had been assigned to her for the duration of her case. It had been Beth who'd stayed with her while the police surgeon had done his work and Beth again who'd taken her statement about the day's events.

When they'd finally brought her to this unexpectedly homely little sitting room she'd offered to bring Abby food and drink. Just the thought of it had made Abby feel sick.

Then she'd tried to talk to her to take her mind off her double ordeal, but all Abby had wanted to do had been to curl up in a corner.

There was a soft tap at the door and out of the corner of her eye she saw the young woman stand to open it. There was the indecipherable sound of a low-voiced conversation and then Beth turned to Abby and beckoned her over.

'They're ready for you now,' she said quietly, and waited for Abby to join her at the door.

Her knees were shaking and she clutched her bag to her like a lifeline as she was ushered along a series of bland corridors and into a darkened room, knowing what was coming next.

She'd been reassured that the sheet of glass in front of her was mirrored on the other side so that the line of men in the brightly lit room couldn't possibly see her. Even so, she found herself cringing back into her chair, her knees shaking too much to hold her up.

Her eyes skated blindly along them, the whole episode feeling slightly surreal—as if she'd just found herself caught up in an episode of a television cops-and-robbers series. She found herself speculating idly how the police had managed to find nearly a dozen men of roughly the same build and colouring at this time of night.

As the senior policeman sat in the chair on the other side of her such inane mental rambling faded.

'You can take your time,' he reminded Abby, his gentle voice at odds with his commanding air. 'You mustn't pick anyone out of the line-up unless you're absolutely certain.'

Abby nodded, clenching her hands together tightly as the trembling intensified, and this time when she looked at the waiting men she forced herself to concentrate on the first face.

She got to the seventh one before her breath stopped in her throat and her heart thumped unevenly.

His mid-brown hair was rumpled, as though he'd run his fingers through it more than once, and his open-necked shirt had the distinctive pleated front that told her he'd actually been in evening dress when he'd been brought in.

A swift stab of jealousy made her wonder who he'd been with, then she remembered what he was capable of and common sense took over again.

It would only be par for the course for him to do something as duplicitous as two-timing her. After all, he was the sort of man who'd do this to her after telling her how much he liked and respected her.

'Well, miss?' the policeman prompted. 'Is he here?'

Abby cast a cursory glance along the rest of the line but there was no real point. She knew who'd done this to her.

'Number seven,' she croaked through a throat swollen almost closed by bruising.

'You're absolutely certain?' he questioned patiently.

'Absolutely,' she confirmed with a nod, unable to take her eyes away.

How could she mistake his face? She saw it nearly every day.

In the last couple of months she'd gone from an instant appreciation of his good-looking brand of sexuality to an overwhelming attraction towards Ben as a doctor and as a man. Her pulse and breathing reacted to nothing more than the thought of him, making the secrecy he'd insisted on at work rather difficult to maintain.

Strangely, the pull didn't seem to be quite as strong when they were out together, and she wondered if it was an example of feminine perversity that she hadn't wanted him quite so much when he hadn't been forbidden fruit.

Whatever the reason, when he'd wrapped her in his

arms to kiss her goodnight at the end of an evening out together she still hadn't found it too difficult to avoid asking him in to spend the night.

She hadn't realised that he didn't share her reticence until he'd—

'Well, then, miss, that's all we need from you at the moment,' someone broke into her darkening thoughts. 'WPC Cassidy will take you home as soon as you're ready. Is there someone you'd like to call before you leave? Someone to keep you company?'

She was listening to what the officer was saying but her eyes were still focused on the brightly lit room on the other side of the glass, watching one particular man as the line turned to file out.

His expression was stony and unreadable—totally unlike anything she'd seen before, even during the attack.

Her mind swiftly skittered away from that image and she concentrated on the present and the person behind the glass. It was amazing how different he looked when he wasn't wearing a collar and tie. She'd noticed it the first time he'd approached her to ask her out, surprised to find that he'd been waiting for her around the corner from the hospital.

He'd always shed some of his commanding persona with his name-tag and had always seemed very keen to please her—until today.

She frowned as she watched him, disturbed by a faint feeling that there was something wrong...something different about him...something not quite right...

She couldn't pinpoint it and it wasn't really important, not in comparison with what he'd done.

Suddenly she was overwhelmed with the need to

know why. 'Wait,' she called to the senior officer's retreating back, and everyone in the room turned to look at her. 'I want to speak to him.'

'That's not a good idea, Miss Walker,' said the slightly scratchy voice of the duty solicitor. 'If, as seems likely, there's going to be a court case then the less the two of you have to do with each other the better. Keep any contact strictly between your solicitors and—'

'Is his solicitor here?' she interrupted impatiently, gripped by the feeling that this was something she *must* do for the sake of her own sanity.

One of the shadowy figures at the back of the room had paused in the doorway and now stepped back into the room.

'Just what are you asking for?' he demanded sharply. 'I can't allow you to do anything to put my client in any further jeopardy.'

'And, on the other hand, I don't have to fear anything further from him with a room full of solicitors and policemen,' Abby pointed out, pathetically grateful to feel some of her old self-confidence returning as she took control of the conversation.

'You can always advise him not to answer my question if it could be…prejudicial, but the idea of the two of us staying away from each other is crazy. We work together every day, for heaven's sake. What are we supposed to do—walk around with our backs turned to each other and our fingers in our ears for the next however many weeks and months?'

Something in the shift of expressions on the man's face suddenly made her wonder if she *would* be working with Ben in the interim. Would he have to be locked up while he waited for the case to come to court? She had no idea.

The heat of challenge died away, her own uncontrollable claustrophobia forcing her to shudder at the thought of anyone being confined to a cell, no matter how heinous their crime. She gestured hopelessly, her emotions churning inside her.

'It's just... I need to feel that I've got some control over my life again... I need to know *why!*'

She was trembling again as she watched the two solicitors conferring on the other side of the room, and wondered how it had come to this.

The last couple of months had been so wonderful, their increasing pleasure in each other's company something she'd never known before.

It hadn't surprised her that the consummate professional she worked with should be so different when they were together away from the hospital, but she'd been surprised that he should be so adamantly opposed to their colleagues knowing that they were going out together.

As recently as a week ago he'd turned down point-blank an invitation to join a group of friends for a social evening. After the weeks they'd been going out together she'd confronted him, asking him if he was ashamed to be seen with her. When he'd said that he didn't want to share her with anyone yet, pleasure had wrapped her heart in warmth.

It had been the same when she'd suggested having their photo taken together. He'd been against it at first but then had given in and joined her in the booth.

He'd surprised her by playing the fool while the shots were taken and she'd been afraid that they'd all been spoiled, but one shot had caught him just right.

Her hands tightened protectively around her bag when she remembered that single photo she had of the two of them together. Something deep inside her didn't want to lose the one tangible piece of evidence she had left of the happy time they'd shared, but she wondered now whether she ought to give it to the police.

Ben had disappeared from view now, but she could still see in her mind's eye the lean planes of his face as it had been before she'd raked her nails down it in desperation.

It had felt dreadful when each of them had been carefully scraped in case there were any skin cells for forensic examination, but not as dreadful as the other samples they'd had to take for DNA testing and cross-matching.

A commotion by the door drew her attention from a series of memories that would make her shudder for ever, and she saw that he'd just entered the room, escorted by yet another policeman.

The half-wary, half-angry way he looked around at the people gathered there reminded her painfully of a wild animal that suddenly realised it had been trapped and was desperately looking for a way out. In spite of everything that had gone before, she found her heart twisting with sympathy.

'Ben, are you *sure* you want to speak to her?' she heard his solicitor say, and she saw his head come up to scan the room for her.

This time the emotion on his face was easy to read—pure anger. She stepped out from behind her own solicitor and the movement brought his gaze to bear on her.

For a second she felt the lash of his fury aimed at

her, but then it seemed as if he focused on her injuries for the first time and his expression changed to one of horror.

'My God…' she heard him gasp as he stepped forward, one hand coming up as if, even from the other side of the room, he could do something to soothe her pain.

A ghastly silence fell as everyone waited to see what would happen next, and into it Abby forced a single word.

'Why?'

The effort strained her bruised throat and pulled at her split lip, making her wince, but suddenly the anger overtook the hurt and the words poured out of her in a jagged stream.

'Why did you do it, Ben? You said you cared about me and God knows you must have known that I was f-falling in love with you. Why couldn't you w-wait? Why did you have to r-rape me?'

Her tentative control was fraying fast and she couldn't stop the single tear that made its way down to the corner of her mouth, where the sting reminded her of the other injuries he'd inflicted on her.

Ben felt as stunned as if he'd been hit by a body blow. It was one thing to hear himself accused of a heinous crime such as rape and to wonder why anyone would lie about such a false allegation, but to be confronted by evidence like this…

He'd been shocked to the core when they'd told him about the accusation being levelled at him, and his anger had been growing steadily in the long hours since. Each indignity he'd had to suffer while the police surgeon collected his samples for DNA testing had flayed his soul, especially when he remembered *who* had made the allegation.

That Abby Walker, a woman he was so attracted to and enjoyed working with, should single him out for such a monstrous lie was beyond his comprehension. How dared she, especially when they both knew there was no way she could prove it?

But this...

The ugliness of her bruised and battered face made him cringe with instinctive sympathy, but it was the pain and misery in her eyes that pulled at him in spite of his anger.

'I *didn't*,' he denied fiercely for at least the twentieth time, everything in him revolted by the very idea of such an act. 'I couldn't have because I've never been in your company except at work.'

'Stop it!' she shouted hoarsely, silencing him with nothing more than the hurt in her voice. 'You *know* that's not true. There's no point in lying.'

As he watched she suddenly scrabbled in her handbag and drew out a small photograph encased in a clear plastic wallet.

'Here,' she said, taking a couple of shaky steps across the silent room, stopping an arm's length away to hold it out towards him. 'There's the proof. How could we have had our photo taken together if we've never been out together?'

Out of the corner of his eye Ben saw his solicitor start forward as if he wanted to intercept the picture, but nothing could stop him from taking it and seeing her so-called proof with his own eyes.

'That's impossible,' he breathed, all the breath frozen in his lungs with the shock of the image in front of him.

Only this evening he'd been wondering how long her hair was and here, in this small photo, was the evidence that it reached well beyond her shoulders in a glorious honeyed mass. The other half of the photo was a complete impossibility because he could see himself staring out at himself when he knew he'd never been there.

'It's not me,' he said, shaking his head in disbelief, an awful sick feeling settling in the pit of his stomach. 'It can't be.'

'Ben, the police have taken samples,' she reminded him hoarsely. 'They're going to be able to match the DNA from the…from your…'

Suddenly she didn't seem to be able to meet his eyes, and he suddenly remembered the series of indignities she'd had to go through while the intimate samples were collected. Then he saw her pull herself together and he was almost proud of the way she could draw on that inner strength of hers.

'They even found some skin cells under my nails from when I scratched you…' She gestured towards him with one hand, and saw her eyes widen as she looked at him again.

She stepped closer, moving as slowly as if he were some sort of dangerous animal who might pounce at any minute, until she stood close enough to gaze up at his face.

'I scratched your cheek,' she said, a puzzled frown pleating her pale forehead. 'There were red marks all the way down.' Her fingertips hovered over her own injured face as she imitated the action. 'You hit me and…and called me a bitch for marking your face…'

She blinked, obviously confused.

'How did you do that?' she whispered. 'It's impossible. It was only hours ago and there isn't a mark on you.'

'That's because it *wasn't* me,' he declared forcefully, a hint of his own monumental anger escaping into his voice while he fought his pity for the poor injured woman. 'I've never touched you.'

CHAPTER TWO

'DO YOU want me to come home with you?' Beth Cassidy asked.

Abby knew she was only doing her job, but the thought of having the young policewoman with her would somehow prolong the whole nightmare. What she really needed was the chance to think everything through for herself.

'I'd rather not, if you don't mind. I...I'll make a phone call...' She paused, not quite certain who she would call. She certainly didn't want anyone at the hospital to find out about this.

'Get one of your friends to stay with you,' the young WPC encouraged. 'If you change your mind and want to talk to me, I'm only on the other end of the phone—day or night.'

Abby felt her strained attempt at a smile stretching the split on her lip and hoped that the other woman was fooled. Suddenly it was very important that she should get away from here. There was a volcanic explosion of emotion building up inside her and she wanted to be on her own if she lost control of it.

She thought longingly of her parents. It would be wonderful to be able to go home and let her mother cosset her the way she had as a child. There had been something special about the feeling which had made it seem as if she'd been protected against the world.

Except that they lived on the other side of the world now, having moved there to be closer to their grandchildren when big brother Jamie had emigrated to New Zealand.

At the time she'd just qualified as a nurse and had waved them off with a smile as she'd contemplated the freedom of living her own life.

Why was it that now she felt as if she'd been abandoned, her problems such that she couldn't possibly talk about them over the phone? She certainly couldn't get a hug that way.

The taxi-driver who arrived in answer to her phone call was one of the regulars at the rank outside the entrance of St Augustine's, and the sight of his familiar, craggy face was the first really ordinary thing that had happened for hours.

She gave him the address of her flat but when he stopped outside she was suddenly frozen, assailed by a kaleidoscope of memories of the events that had taken place in her flat.

Her pulse started to race and her breathing grew ragged, her hands shaking so badly that she couldn't even make herself reach for the handle to open the door.

'On second thoughts,' she mumbled, furious at her own cowardice, 'could you take me to a small local bed-and-breakfast place?'

He turned to look at her over his shoulder when she made no attempt to leave the cab, and she saw the flash of compassion soften his face.

'I know just the place,' he said cheerfully, and began to chatter as if he knew she needed something to take her mind off her own thoughts. 'It's not far from here and very clean. I recommend it to people who want to stay close by when there's a member of their family in the hospital. The rooms are small but Mrs

Halloran, the landlady, is accustomed to being woken up at all hours and she's always got a supply of essentials like soap and toothpaste on hand…'

Abby let his gravelly voice roll over her as he negotiated the turns to a road very much like her own and drew up in front of a typical Victorian three-storey house.

'It'll all look better in the morning, lass,' he added softly, as he hurried to open the door for her and held it wide, a courtesy she'd never received from a taxi-driver before.

'I hope so,' Abby replied with a shaky smile, suddenly conscious that she was staying as far away from the poor man as possible—as if the whole episode had been something to do with him. 'It couldn't get much worse.'

'Don't you believe it,' he said, his voice suddenly very serious. 'Bruises fade and so do the sharp edges on memories. At least you can be glad you're alive.'

His words seemed to hang in the dark quietness, the yellow punctuation marks of streetlights highlighting his face to reveal a sadness that she was certain he usually hid under his jovial personality.

'You're quite right,' Abby said, ashamed that she'd allowed her misery to preoccupy her to the exclusion of everything else. Bad as her experience had been, there were plenty of things that could have happened to her that would have been far worse. She ought to know—she saw any number of them on a daily basis in the accident and emergency department at St Augustine's.

'I can't guarantee that I'll ever be able to look back on this and laugh,' she added, straightening her shoulders and conscious that her chin had come up, 'but, as you say, at least I'll be alive to look back on it.'

'That's the spirit,' he said encouragingly. 'Now, you go and ring on the bell and get yourself a good night's sleep. It's amazing what you can face the next day.'

Two days later Abby still hadn't been able to force herself to go back into her flat, but she hadn't been able to bear sitting in her little rented bedroom any longer.

It was every bit as clean as the taxi-driver had promised and Mrs Halloran was every bit as welcoming, but she wasn't used to idleness and with recent events playing on her mind...

To stop herself reliving the trauma over and over again Abby was desperate enough to try to watch an indigestible diet of daytime soaps, but she found the plots and characters too far-fetched to hold her attention.

Halfway through the third day she barely restrained herself from screaming with frustration and throwing something at the prettily papered walls. Knowing that she needed to find something to occupy her hands and her mind if she wasn't to go round the bend, she phoned the hospital instead.

'Are you sure you're ready to come back?' she was asked with obvious concern. 'You know, you can take as much time as you need.'

'Yes, I'm sure,' she replied fervently, grateful that her superior couldn't see her crossed fingers.

It wasn't that all her injuries had completely healed—she still bore visible marks of her ordeal on her face that might invite questions. Even so, she was confident that a little extra make-up would hide those sufficiently that they wouldn't cause too much speculation. It was the other, less visible injuries that were the problem.

She'd already found that her enforced break left her with too little to do and too much time for thinking and remembering.

Even after three days she wasn't eating properly and still hadn't been able to sleep for more than an hour before the nightmare woke her up. If she was lucky, going back to work would at least make her tired enough that she could have an unbroken night.

It was only when she paused by the door to the A and E department the next day to draw in a steadying breath and smooth trembling hands down over her uniform that she finally admitted the truth that had haunted her every waking and sleeping moment—how was she going to cope with coming face to face with Ben for the first time?

'Hello, Abby. Feeling better?' asked a softly accented Scottish voice as she emerged into the department.

She turned to face diminutive Senior Sister Celia MacDonald with her first genuine smile in days. Trust Big Mac to be in exactly the right place at the right time. The woman's instincts really were uncanny.

'Yes, Sister,' she answered promptly, suddenly feeling far more confident than she had just a minute ago. She knew that her superior wouldn't have been told about what had happened—that was confidential—but she also knew that the older woman was extremely intelligent and had been doing her job for a long time.

It was quite likely that she had put two and two together and had come very close to the correct total, but as she could never be accused of gossiping Abby was certain that it wouldn't go any further.

'Good,' she said, with her characteristic nod of approval. 'But if you find yourself...flagging at any stage I'll expect you to let me know.'

That was obviously all she wanted to say before she whisked off across the department, but it was enough to tell Abby that the indomitable woman would be keeping a friendly eye on her and genuinely cared about her.

'Hey, Abby. Sorry to hear about your accident. Are you OK?' Tina Wadland called as she caught sight of her.

For a moment Abby stiffened with dread at the prospect of a quizzing, but then she remembered that the story the staff had been given for her unexpected absence was that she'd had a bad fall.

'I'm fine. Just a bit bruised,' she said lightly, as she turned towards the younger woman. Behind the junior's head another taller figure turned to face her, and when her eyes met Ben's intent hazel gaze across the room her voice froze in her throat.

For a moment it felt as if her heart had stopped beating, then it raced on at a frantic pace as remembered terror rose up to suffocate her.

Something of her feelings must have shown on her face because suddenly she saw a searing expression of pain in his eyes. It was quickly hidden behind lowered lids, and when he looked up again to greet her with a silent nod it had completely disappeared.

Big Mac's calm voice, calling Tina across to attend to a minor casualty, broke the tension of the moment, but it took Abby longer than that to get her pulse and breathing under control again. She was almost grateful for the distraction of caring for a child with a bad gash on his leg.

Even so, her mind seemed to be operating on two separate levels.

One part of her was asking questions about the camp the youngster had been building on waste ground near his home and the jagged piece of glass he'd fallen on. The other part was bewailing the fact that, in spite of the many hours that had passed, she still hadn't been ready for her first meeting with Ben.

There had been no warning—she hadn't even known he'd been in the room until their eyes had met. At least if she'd heard his voice or someone had spoken to him she'd have been able to... What? Put on a suit of armour? As if *that* would have made any difference.

She'd had four days now to prepare herself for the first time she saw him since their confrontation at the police station. Four days in which he'd been part of every thought she'd had, every dream she'd suffered.

Now he was standing just inches away as he looked closely at the angry-looking gash in the skinny leg between them, and she was hard-pushed not to shy away from any contact with him.

'Aren't you being brave?' she exclaimed brightly, as she covered the youngster's wound again with the temporary dressing, grateful that the quivering deep inside her wasn't visible in her hands.

As it was, she had to perform the task one-handed as her other hand was tightly clenched in the child's grubby paw.

'What's he going to do to it?' the youngster demanded in a fearful whisper, the shaky sound of his voice telling her that he wasn't far from tears. His eyes were fixed on the tall figure speaking to his parents, almost as if he were expecting him to suddenly grow fangs. 'I—I won't have to have an operation, will I? I don't want to go un-unconshus or he might cut my leg off.'

'No! Nothing like that!' Abby exclaimed, with a reassuring laugh. 'All they'll do is stitch that nasty cut up to stop all your blood leaking out. It's not a *real* operation.'

'So I won't have to go un-conshus?' he pressed awkwardly. 'Will I be awake while they sew me up?' He didn't look as if he relished that option either.

'Well, it will take a long time to do all the stitches in a big cut like that, and it gets very boring for you to try to keep still for a long time so they'll probably let you have a bit of a sleep before they start.'

Abby was mentally crossing her fingers while she spoke to him, torn between trying to allay his fears and giving him more information than she could reasonably assume. She didn't actually know what Ben had decided was necessary, but when the youngster started getting agitated she'd had to make an educated guess.

While he'd been examining the wound she'd caught Ben's muttered comments about the depth of the laceration and the fact that it would be better if the closure was done under anaesthetic in Theatre.

In spite of her aversion to Ben's proximity, she'd found herself watching him while he'd made his examination to pick up clues as to the severity of the injury. She'd gathered that he didn't think there had been any damage to nerves or blood vessels but, unfortunately, the edges of the wound were very jagged.

Abby knew from seeing many similar wounds that

he would be worried that by the time the tattered skin had been neatened it would have to be stretched very tightly for the edges to meet. It might even need a skin graft to close it.

She also knew that was the *last* thing the child needed to hear.

Out of the corner of her eye she saw that Ben had finished speaking to the youngster's parents, and marvelled at the change in their expressions.

Just a few minutes ago they had looked quite grey with fear, but now, although they had a little more colour in their faces as they approached their son, Abby could see that they were still anticipating his reaction when he heard what was going to happen to him.

'Are you all right?' the young woman asked as she hurried to his side, and Abby saw the way her eyes were drawn to the young lad's grip on her hand.

'I'm not frightened any more,' he announced with a seven-year-old's bravado. 'The nurse told me I didn't have to have an operation on my leg.'

'Oh, but the doctor said...' his mother began, and Abby's heart sank a little when she saw the swift scowl that drew Ben's straight, dark brows together.

'She told me that they're going to stitch it all up,' he continued, blithely oblivious to the consternation around him, 'and she said it gets very boring and difficult because I would have to stay very still for a long time so the doctor will let me have a bit of a sleep while they do it.'

Abby drew in a relieved breath when she saw the way Ben's expression lightened at the child's explanation, and her heartbeat evened out again.

'Well, then, young man, shall I tell them to get

ready for you?' Ben asked with a smile and a quizzical lift of an eyebrow.

'Can Mum and Dad come with me?' he asked, with a momentary return of nervousness.

'Of course they can. We'll put them to work, pushing you along the corridor, shall we?'

Not long after that Abby waved them on their way along the first of several corridors in the maze that was St Augustine's, then reminded herself that it was time to complete the task of clearing the cubicle ready for its next occupant.

'Abby.'

She hadn't realised that Ben was standing behind her so when she turned round she almost collided with him.

'Ben...'

She gulped and took a hasty step backwards. Too nervous to wait to hear what he had to say, she hurried past him, taking great care not to get close enough for him to touch her.

For a moment she stood in the cubicle, dreading the thought that he might follow her. Her heart was beating so fast that she felt quite light-headed. Suddenly she remembered the time she'd rescued a bird from a cat. As she'd cradled the fragile thing in her hands she'd felt its tiny heart beating faster and faster until, to her shock, it had stopped altogether.

'Scared to death,' she whispered, the old memory making her sad all over again.

The comparison she was drawing between herself and a baby bird suddenly struck her as absurd and she snorted in self-derision.

'Well, I'm no fragile bird and I'm not going to let it get to me,' she muttered under her breath, as she smoothed another length of disposable paper sheeting over the bed and gave a last glance around the cubicle.

In spite of her resolution, she still found herself glancing both ways along the wide corridor before she set off, glad that it would soon be time for her break.

Two youngsters were racing about among the chairs, completely ignoring the older woman who was trying to persuade them to sit still. Abby felt like going over and giving the young tearaways a piece of her mind, but just then they were offered a bribe of a drink and they bounded away like exuberant puppies.

It could only have been a matter of seconds later that there was the sound of a crash and a shriek, and Abby took off at a rapid walk.

Right at the entrance of the coffee-shop run by volunteers lay the older woman, with her leg twisted at an awkward angle. She was surrounded by the debris from a small tray, and the widening orange puddle to one side of her marked the fate of the orange juice she'd chosen for the two boys.

Far more serious was the spreading brown stain on her pretty blouse where her cup of freshly poured tea or coffee must have landed.

With a speed born of experience Abby grabbed the plastic beaker the volunteer had just poured for the next customer in line and dashed the contents over the steaming fabric.

'Lie still, my love,' she advised, one hand resting on the struggling woman's shoulder. 'That'll take a bit of the heat out of it until we can get you into a cubicle, but it looks as if you've hurt your leg.'

'I don't know which hurts worse, the spilt coffee or my leg,' she muttered through gritted teeth. 'I feel so stupid.'

'Those young idiots knocked her over,' accused a bystander, with a glare at a very chastened pair.

Abby had guessed that was what had happened, but she was too concerned with organising the poor woman's transfer to a cubicle to spare them more than a glance.

By the time she'd removed the coffee-soaked clothing and applied Water Jel dressings to take out the heat, Ben had arrived to take a look at her.

'It's not broken, is it?' she asked fearfully. 'I'm looking after the children for my daughter. She had to come here because she tripped over the boys' skateboard and broke her arm. They're putting a plaster on it.'

'Well, I'm afraid this leg's broken, too,' Ben told her, and when she began to cry he took hold of her hand and patted it until she regained control.

'I'm sorry, Doctor,' she sniffed, and blew her nose on the paper hankie he offered her. 'Am I going to have a plaster cast, too?'

'I'm afraid so. You might even have to stay in hospital for a couple of days while we sort you out,' he warned.

'Oh, but I can't!' she exclaimed, obviously horrified. 'My daughter's relying on me to help her out while her arm mends. She won't be able to do much cooking and cleaning with her arm in plaster.'

'In which case, it's going to be up to these two to make amends,' Ben pointed out grimly, his expression fierce as he glared at the two boys standing at the end of the bed.

They'd been fidgeting ever since they'd followed their grandmother into the cubicle. Their eyes and fingers would have been everywhere if Abby hadn't been keeping an eagle eye on them.

Under Ben's ferocious frown they became miraculously still, their eyes widening as he stalked across to them.

Abby had the feeling that he'd done it deliberately when she saw the way he was looming over them, and had to suppress a wicked smile. It was no more than they deserved, by all accounts.

'So,' Ben began in a very serious voice, 'I understand the two of you left your skateboard out so your mother fell and broke her arm?'

The two glanced at each other then looked back up at Ben and nodded silently.

'And now you've knocked your grandmother over and broken her leg and scalded her with boiling coffee?' he persisted.

Their eyes were widening with every second as they nodded again.

'Well, then, it seems to me that if it's all your fault that the two of them are going to be in plaster for weeks, the only fair thing would be if the two of you take over all your mum's jobs until she's well again. Do you agree?'

The nods were slower in coming this time as the enormity of what had happened began to dawn on them.

'How?' the braver of the two croaked. 'We can't do the cooking in the oven. Mum and Nanna say it's too dangerous.'

'But you're certainly old enough to put your toys away, make the beds, hoover the carpets and do the washing-up,' Ben pointed out firmly. 'Do you agree, Nanna?'

'Well, they are six and five years old now,' she confirmed, and Abby marvelled at how much less anxious she looked now that Ben had taken a hand in the situation. The pain relief he'd given her was probably part of the reason, but his ingenious idea for punishment had obviously struck a chord with her. 'I think it would be a very good idea.'

There was a commotion just outside the cubicle and a flustered-looking woman hurried in.

'Oh, Mum, what happened? Are you hurt?' she cried, her plastered arm residing in a pristine sling.

It only took a few succinct sentences for Ben to bring her up to date on the catastrophic events of the last half-hour. By the time he'd extracted promises from the two youngsters to take care of their mum and nanna, it was time for the older woman to be taken for X-rays.

For Abby it was time to clear away the debris and prepare the cubicle for the next patient. Then, thankfully, she was due for a break.

Ten minutes later she was slumped in one of the squashy chairs grouped round a low coffee-table, surrounded by a motley assortment of colleagues.

Their drinks were contained in anything from an aluminium can straight from the refrigerated dispenser out in the main concourse to a selection of mugs, cups and glasses.

Some of them were taking advantage of the break to wolf down a sandwich or two while others were passing round a large packet of chocolate digestive biscuits.

'Hey, Maurice! Don't be greedy!' the owner of the packet called indignantly. 'That's three you've taken!'

'They're stuck together so it counts as one,' the

older man retorted with a wicked grin, and took a quick bite when it looked as if she was going to get up to relieve him of them.

The packet arrived in front of Abby but she waved it past, still not really interested in eating...not really interested in much at all beyond the endless rerunning of her own thoughts.

'Are you sure you're all right?' Tina asked quietly.

The soft-voiced question drew Abby away from her introspection. She'd hardly noticed the younger woman as she sat there, a member of the group but not really part of it.

'I *will* be,' she replied equally softly. Her pulse rate doubled at the question and she was glad that her colleague was being discreet.

The last thing she wanted was to become the centre of attention for the whole group. She didn't think she could manage to field very many questions about her fictitious fall without raising a few suspicions. The staff in an A and E department heard too many 'I walked into a door' explanations from battered wives not to spot a phony story.

'Well, I suppose it was one way of getting a few extra days off,' Tina teased wryly. 'Did you manage to make a start on that decorating you were talking about?'

For a moment Abby couldn't think what she was talking about, her whole attention suddenly drawn to the man who had just walked through the door.

Was he following her, for heaven's sake? It seemed as if every time she turned round there he was.

'Actually, I wasn't feeling much like it,' she said with hidden irony, knowing that she hadn't even felt like walking through the front door yet, let alone thought about starting to decorate.

She'd watched Ben surreptitiously while Tina had tried to draw her into the general conversation going on around her, but the whole while she'd been afraid that he was going to come over to speak to her.

Her reaction to him was hard enough to control when he was busy looking after a patient. How she would cope when there could be any number of eyes watching them, ever-eager to glean some small item to send around the hospital grapevine, didn't bear thinking about.

Finally, she saw someone buttonhole him and seized her chance to escape. She couldn't help a small grimace of sympathy when she overheard part of the conversation and realised the grey-haired gentleman was bending Ben's ear about some of the finer points of hospital politics.

Her return to duty coincided with the arrival of a young soldier home on leave to visit his girlfriend.

'I took her out for a meal to celebrate,' he told Abby, his pale face sheened with sweat as he sat on the edge of the bed with his arms wrapped tightly around his waist. 'A proper meal at a hotel, not just a bar meal in a pub. I was going to propose to her at the end of the meal, but then I didn't feel very well and when I went to the toilets I was very sick.'

He looked up at her with his eyes full of fear as he continued, 'I brought up blood.'

'Why didn't you go to your doctor last night, then?' Abby asked, wondering why the young man had waited so long before seeking attention.

'He's the medical officer at camp, and I'm not due back for a couple more days,' he explained. 'I didn't want to worry my girlfriend or her family by asking who their GP was, but I didn't feel happy about putting it off any longer…just in case it's something serious.'

Abby took careful note of what he'd eaten for his last few meals in case he was suffering from food poisoning or an allergy, but it was the mention of blood that had her worried.

'Isn't he young to have an ulcer?' she asked quietly when she reported her findings to Ben. She was pleased to note that this time she seemed to have her response to him under rather better control. Perhaps it was the fact that most of her concentration was on the pale young man waiting in the cubicle.

'Not necessarily,' Ben replied thoughtfully. 'You said he's in the army, which means he'll have regularly eaten in less than pristine conditions, probably in some of the less salubrious parts of the world.'

'What difference does that make?' she demanded. 'I know the troops can get pitchforked into dangerous situations at a moment's notice, but would that cause enough stress to give him ulcers like a middle-aged tycoon?'

'Unlikely,' he agreed, 'but it could mean he's been infected with Helicobacter pylori. That could give him all the same symptoms and, in the end, do even more damage.'

Abby stood quietly by while Ben conducted his examination of the young man, and wasn't surprised when it seemed as if his instinctive reaction had been right. She marvelled again at just how wide a range of knowledge an A and E physician had to have. Patients with any condition could walk in through those doors, and they all expected him to be able to deal with it.

'So what can I do about it?' the young soldier asked, his face even more worried now than before. 'Will this mean I have to leave the army?'

'Not at all,' Ben replied easily, as he began to fill in the requisite forms. 'These days it's easy enough to test and the treatment is equally simple—just a week's course of three different antibiotics taken as a special cocktail.'

'And that cures it?' He sounded understandably sceptical.

'If that's what you've got, I can almost guarantee it,' Ben said with a smile. 'In no time at all you'll be tucking into your favourite biryani and vindaloo.'

A pained expression crossed his boyish face and his muscular arms tightened around his stomach.

'I think I'll give that a miss for a while, if you don't mind. I can't even face the thought of spicy food at the moment.' He paused for a moment. 'But what if it isn't that heleo-whatever?'

'In that case, if the tests don't give us any other clues you'll probably need to have an endoscopy—a thin tube with a miniature camera goes down into your stomach for a look-see.'

'Would I have to come back here for that? Only I'm due back at camp soon and I won't be getting much leave for several weeks.'

'Don't worry about that,' Ben reassured him. 'Sister here will give you the details of your hospital reference number and your MO back at the base can get all the information sent straight to him. He'll be able to update your records and take everything from there.'

Ben made hurried farewells when Big Mac's head appeared round the curtain to request his urgent attention for an accident victim due any moment, and Abby found herself drawing a silent breath of relief.

It wasn't long before she was directing a very relieved young man through the department with instructions to stick to a fairly bland diet for the next few days. Then it was time to clear the cubicle again ready for the next occupant and she was alone with her thoughts once more.

Tina's reminder that she had things to take care of at her flat had preyed on Abby's mind all day, and finally forced her into the decision to return home that night.

She'd been away for days now, and the food in her fridge had been there so long that it had probably mutated into alien life-forms. 'Apart from anything else, I need to do something about my laundry basket,' she muttered under her breath as she walked briskly back out into the department. 'I can't afford to buy new clothes just because I can't face going in there.'

Later, as she was walking along in the gathering dusk towards the familiar late-Victorian building, she found her steps slowing with dread.

She'd already delayed her homecoming by a couple of hours with a protracted shopping trip. She knew the contents of her fridge, vegetable rack and fruit bowl were going to be useless, and the results of her spending spree were weighing her down on both sides.

The last few yards seemed to stretch into infinity and her feet moved as slowly as if she were wading through treacle until she realised what she was doing to herself.

'It won't get any better if you put it off,' she muttered fiercely under her breath, and shoved the gate open with her elbow, grateful for once that the last person through it hadn't closed the latch properly.

The next problem was finding her key, and she concentrated on piling her purchases on the top step before she fished in the bottom of her bag—anything to take her mind off the last time she'd let herself in through this door.

As she ferried the bags into the hallway she reminded herself that she hadn't latched the gate either, and she reached out with one hand to switch on the light against the gathering gloom as she reached back to pluck the key out of the lock.

'Abby?' said a deep voice, and suddenly Ben appeared in the doorway, silhouetted against the last of the dying light.

With her recurring nightmare still so fresh in her mind, this exact re-enactment of the events of that night were too much for her. With her heart hammering in her throat, Abby let loose a blood-curdling scream.

CHAPTER THREE

'ABBY! For heaven's sake!' Ben exclaimed, the expression on his face full of horror at the violence of her reaction. The quick glance that he sent over his shoulder at the neighbouring houses made him look haunted and hunted. 'I only want to talk to you!'

'Talk?' she echoed breathlessly, barely able to utter a word as her heart tried to batter its way out of her chest.

Inside her head she was reliving that dreadful moment when, instead of swinging shut, her front door had burst inwards under the forceful thrust of a male hand and she'd been knocked to the floor by the impact.

'Abby?'

It was the concern in his voice that penetrated her blind panic and enabled her to make herself look at him properly.

As she'd feared, it was Ben who was standing there, but this time, although he'd reached one hand out towards her, he'd made no attempt to come into the house.

'Wh-what are you doing here?' she demanded, a betraying quiver in her voice 'Y-you're not supposed to come near me out of work. The police said. It—it's breaking the conditions of your bail.'

'That's what I came to tell you,' he said, his quiet voice just as soothing on her ragged nerves as it was when he used it on one of his patients. 'The police have been trying to reach you to let you know the results of the tests.'

'Tests?' she parroted, hardly able to think coherently.

'The fingerprints. Remember?'

Abby remembered.

The fact that she'd never invited Ben into her flat had meant that there had only been the one opportunity for him to leave any prints there, but he *had* handled that little photograph. He'd actually been going to take it out of the protective sleeve when she'd shown it to him, but she'd whisked it out of his hands in case he didn't let her have it back.

Detective Constable Sharp had looked quite delighted when she'd told him about it, but she'd been surprised at the pang she'd felt when she'd watched him slip it into an evidence bag to send it off to be dusted for prints.

'What did they find?' she asked quietly.

She was still clinging onto the door, not quite certain whether her legs would hold her, and every inch of her body seemed to be acutely aware of the distance between the two of them.

She could tell from the way he was holding himself that the news he carried was good from his point of view. He could have let the police catch up with her, but he'd obviously needed to tell her himself.

'They didn't match,' he said, his hazel eyes gazing directly at her.

Abby was silent for a moment as she took in the information, surprised that his expression was one of sympathy rather than the residual anger she would have expected.

An accusation such as the one she'd made against

him could have been enough to ruin his career, even if it had been made purely maliciously. In her case—

Suddenly another thought hit her with the force of a thunderbolt.

'But if it wasn't you...' she whispered, then couldn't complete the thought.

She could feel the blood draining away from her face, and there was a high-pitched singing noise in her ears as everything began to grow hazy.

'Abby!'

She heard Ben's exclamation, but it seemed to be coming from a long way away...

'It's all right, I've got you,' murmured a deep voice in her ear, as she swam up towards the surface again.

Abby stiffened.

It was the voice from her nightmares, and it was actually in the room with her again. His hand was on her shoulder, preventing her from getting up.

'No! Don't hurt me,' she moaned, and struggled weakly against his grasp. 'Please, don't hurt me.'

Suddenly the hand was gone.

'I wouldn't hurt you, Abby,' Ben said quietly, his own hurt evident in his voice, and deep inside her she knew it was true.

She'd seen the gentle way he treated all his patients, no matter how young or old, and no matter how out of control he might get in the throes of desire, she couldn't imagine that he would ever resort to violence to get what he wanted.

But if that was true... If Ben was a trustworthy man...

'Who was it?' she whispered, taking the next logical step as she opened her eyes and stared straight up into his, fear putting a quiver in her voice. 'If it wasn't you, who was it?'

Suddenly she couldn't bear being in such a vulnerable position any more and struggled to get up.

'Take it slowly,' he advised, one hand held out protectively towards her as if he was afraid she might keel over again.

Abby was glad he didn't try to touch her again. At the moment it felt as if every nerve ending was screaming with awareness of how close he was.

It was a relief to be on her feet again, even though she still felt shaky. And while she couldn't feel relaxed in his company, she needed something to do to occupy her hands.

'Can I get you a drink?' she offered, all at once the perfect hostess.

'I'd rather you sat down and let me get you something,' he countered. 'You still look very pale.'

She didn't want a drink, didn't think she'd be able to swallow a mouthful while the awful possibilities were swirling inside her head.

Numbly she shook her head, and led the way across to the two chairs facing each other at the end of her minute sitting room. Her knees were distinctly shaky by the time she lowered herself into one of them and gestured towards the other.

'Abby, now that you know it wasn't me we need to talk about who it *was*,' he began quietly, typically getting right to the heart of the matter.

For a moment Abby was silent as she gathered her whirling thoughts into some sort of order.

'I was so certain,' she said at last. 'I was so shocked that you would… I suppose I just saw what I expected to see… No, not *expected* because I didn't expect anything like that... Oh, I don't know what I'm trying to say,' she ended in exasperation.

'Did you see the face of the man who attacked you clearly?' he asked.

'Yes,' she replied instantly, then paused and thought again. 'At least... Now that I think of it... I was just shutting the door and I was reaching for the light switch at the same time.' She concentrated for a moment as she tried to get the sequence of events absolutely clear in her mind.

'So when he pushed the door open...' Ben prompted, his elbows planted on his thighs as he leaned towards her. His hazel eyes were almost mesmerising in their intensity as he willed her to remember.

'It was dark outside and dark inside and he was just a silhouette in the doorway,' she confirmed, describing the images imprinted in her memory.

'So it could have been anyone, waiting in the shadows by the gatepost?' he asked. 'Like I was tonight?'

'Except the voice seemed to be the same at first, but when I scratched you...him...' She shook her head. 'Then the voice changed—it almost became a different person's—and you...*he* was so angry and I'd never heard you say words like that but I was so certain that it was...or I'd never have said it was... I wouldn't make a false accusation against someone I cared about,' she ended hotly, angered by her own inability to say what she meant.

'Well, thank you for those few kind words,' he said, and she was startled to realise that he was actually trying to tease her.

Suddenly she realised just what she'd admitted to, and she felt the heat of a blush creep up her throat.

As if she didn't have enough problems with everything going on in her life at the moment.

'As I see it, that leaves us with a couple of questions to answer,' he said, leaning back in his chair and reverting to his more serious mood. Abby breathed a sigh of relief that he didn't seem to have picked up on her slip. 'Firstly, there's the possibility that the person who attacked you is some sort of stalker who took advantage of the fact that your date had left you at the door without making sure you'd shut it safely.'

He paused, obviously wanting her comments on his suggestion.

'I suppose it could have been,' she said slowly, trying to fit in his theory with the events of that night. 'But that means that whoever it was knows where I live and he could…' The ramifications of that thought were too terrible to voice aloud.

She stared slowly around the room that had been her little haven ever since she'd moved to St Augustine's, and realised that it didn't feel the same any more.

She'd been so proud of her first real home of her own and had slowly collected the furniture and furnishings until she had it just the way she wanted it.

Now it would be forever tainted by the violence that had exploded its peaceful atmosphere. She couldn't even force herself to look towards the door leading to her bedroom.

'And the second possibility?' she asked, silently cursing the shaky voice that revealed how close she was to losing her grip. She'd never been a weak, helpless sort of woman and had no intention of becoming one now—especially not in front of *him*.

'That one is rather in the realms of fiction, I'm

afraid, and depends on there being someone around who looks enough like me to pretend he *is* me—although why anyone would want to do that I've no idea,' he added with a frown.

For a moment Abby almost pointed out the fact that she knew him well enough from working with him not to be fooled by an impostor. Then she remembered the news he'd brought her this evening—the fingerprint evidence that *proved* that Ben Taylor hadn't been the man she'd gone out with—and she didn't need to examine his unmarked cheek to quash her earlier belief.

'But if it wasn't you, who was it?' she demanded in frustration. 'The solicitor said you were an only child without any brothers or cousins who could be mistaken for you, but the man I met could almost have been your identical twin. There's no way you couldn't know if you've got a—'

The arrested expression on his face brought her words to a halt.

'What is it?'

'Just a minute.' He held up one lean hand, his hazel eyes darkening as his focus turned inward the way it did when he was concentrating on a problem at work. 'You said he was almost identical? What differences did you notice? Anything...no matter how small or inconsequential.'

He was leaning forward again, his gaze centred intently on her as if he were willing her to remember something that would solve the mystery.

'Well, nothing, really,' she began, at a loss as to what he wanted from her, 'otherwise I *would* have realised that there were two different people. Obviously, his name is Ben and he's the same height and build as you are and his colouring's the same...' She shrugged helplessly.

'*Exactly* the same?' he challenged.

'Yes...well, no. At least...you...*he* seemed to change when you were off duty.'

'Change? In what way?' He seemed to have decided to ignore her confusion over who she was referring to and focus solely on the information he wanted.

'Well, at St Augustine's you're always very much the professional in your dress and your manner...everything. Oh, you're very good with the patients, but there's a sort of...distance between you and the rest of the world, almost as if you're observing us. It makes you seem more imposing...more aloof.'

She saw him frown again and she was almost certain that there was an element of hurt there, too, before she dragged her eyes away and hurried into speech again.

'Off duty, you were much more relaxed and casual and you absolutely refused to speak about anything to do with work. After that first time you even insisted on meeting me away from the hospital so our colleagues wouldn't see us together. You said it was better that way until we were ready to let them know how we felt about each other...about our relationship...'

She suddenly heard what she was saying and she could have curled into a ball with embarrassment.

'I mean, *he*...' she began, cursing her runaway tongue as she felt the heat scorch her face.

'I know what you meant,' he said, his voice calm and far softer than she'd expected. 'For however many weeks it was, you thought you were going out with me so it must be difficult to make the mental switch now that you know it wasn't. As for the twin theory—'

'I know it's crazy,' she broke in. 'No one could grow up without knowing that they had a twin.'

'They could if they'd been separated and adopted,' Ben pointed out.

'Logically, I suppose that's true,' she conceded. 'But in your own case your parents would have known if they were expecting twins and there would be very little chance that one of them could have been stolen away for adoption without something being said.'

'That would be true, Abby, except for one fact. My parents were never able to have children of their own.'

'But you—'

'Apparently, they were desperate enough to try any avenue, even private, unofficial channels, and when the woman who carried me named her price I was handed over to them when I was just a few minutes old.'

'You were adopted?' This was something that she hadn't even guessed at, and it opened up a whole new range of possibilities. 'Do you know anything about your birth mother? Who she was? Where she came from? Whether you had any siblings?'

'All I knew when I was growing up was what my parents told me—that my mother couldn't keep me and so she gave me up to people who could afford to.'

'Is there any way of finding out any more details? Whether you have any relatives or even a twin?'

'It's unlikely I'll ever be able to find out after all these years.'

'Anyway, I thought adoption agencies insisted on placing twins together.'

'I believe they do now that there's been so much more research into intangible things like sibling bonds, but years ago that might not have been the case. And, apart from the fact that so many years have gone by, I got the feeling, when I last brought the matter up, that there might have been something slightly irregular in my adoption. If so, that would make it even more difficult to trace.'

'But you must be able to do *something*,' she exclaimed heatedly. 'This is the first feasible lead we've come up with.'

'Apart from the unidentified stalker,' he reminded her.

'Who might or might not exist,' she pointed out just as quickly. 'And even if he does that still doesn't explain who the person is who's going round pretending to be you.'

'You're quite right.' Ben sighed and rubbed both hands over his face. 'I'll have another word with my parents and see if we can find some way of getting the old records unlocked. In the meantime, we're both due on duty first thing in the morning so I'd better let you get your shopping put away so you can get ready for bed.'

With just that one sentence the nightmare all came flooding back.

One moment she'd been searching her brain for ways to find out who could possibly be impersonating Ben and the next she was standing in the middle of her diminutive sitting room, and all she could think about was what had happened to her the last time she was in her flat.

'Abby. Are you all right?'

The way he said it told her that it wasn't the first time he'd spoken, but it still didn't make it any easier to swallow the fear-induced tightness in her throat to answer him.

'Dammit, woman, you've gone as white as a sheet. What's the matter with you?' Ben growled, and before she could draw another breath he'd bent and swept her up into his arms.

'Ben!' she squeaked on a gasp of surprise as he turned and marched back towards her tiny hallway as if she weighed little more than a child. 'Put me down!'

'No way. You're so shaky that if I put you down you'll fall down. Where's your bedroom?'

He was carrying her with the utmost care, cradling her against his chest with arms that scarcely seemed to notice the burden, but suddenly the similarities with the other night overwhelmed her and she began to struggle.

'No, Ben. Don't. Put me down,' she pleaded hoarsely, wriggling ineffectually against him.

'Abby...' He tightened his grip on her as if afraid that he might drop her, but all it did was draw her attention to his effortless strength.

She could hear his heart beating fiercely against her face where it was pressed against him—it was almost as fast as her own—but she also knew that she was under his control and blind panic set in.

'No, no,' she wailed through escalating sobs, flailing her legs and flapping her arms. 'Let me go, Ben, let me go. Don't take me in there. Please, don't hurt me. Please...'

His arms froze around her and he stopped walking as suddenly as if he'd walked into a brick wall.

'Abby?' he said, his voice hoarse with the same disbelief she saw in the face above hers.

'Oh, my God,' he breathed, and she knew that he'd

finally realised why she was so terrified. Moving very slowly, as if she were a container of explosive liquid, he released his hold on her and set her on her feet.

Abby was still trying to control her ragged breathing as she watched him take a careful step back from her, but there was nothing she could do about the trickle of tears streaming down her cheeks.

'Do you want me to go?' he asked quietly. 'I'll leave now if you want me to—if you'd rather be alone.'

Abby thought about being shut in her flat by herself and the idea was even worse than having him here with her.

'No,' she said quickly. Too quickly.

The expression on his face told her that she was going to have to explain, especially after her fit of hysterics just now.

'I'm sorry about...' She gestured helplessly, hoping he'd understand 'I'm not really... It's the first time I've been back since...and I haven't really had time to...'

'Where have you been staying? None of your friends seemed to know and no one knew where your family lives.' He sounded almost accusatory—almost as if he'd been worried about her—but she knew it must have been her imagination. After the trouble her allegation must have stirred up for him he'd probably been glad she wasn't around.

'I've been staying in a little bed-and-breakfast place a couple of streets away. I...I couldn't face the idea of coming back here... I didn't know how much the other residents had heard, and the idea of having to tell anyone...'

She heard a pathetic tone creeping into her voice

and a surge of anger made her dredge her sense of self-worth up from the depths.

She straightened her shoulders and lifted her head with new determination. 'I had to come back here today because I've run out of clean clothes. Apart from the fact that my bank balance won't stand too much of the high life—my landlady's been trying to pamper me with breakfast in bed.'

'Would it make things any easier if I helped you get things straight?' he offered, his eyes taking in the tell-tale grey smudges that were the evidence of the scene-of-crime officer's diligence in hunting for fingerprints. 'I won't offer to do your laundry or put your shopping away, but I've been told I make a good cup of tea and I've even been known to lend a hand with washing up and wiping down paintwork.'

As incongruous as the idea was of Dr Ben Taylor helping her to set her flat to rights, it was better than trying to do it with only her memories for company.

'Those are very dangerous admissions,' she said, with the first beginnings of a smile as a soft warmth began to spread through her. Her voice gradually gained strength as she went on. 'So dangerous that I think I ought to put them to the test—starting with the tea-making.'

'I am yours to command,' he said, with a smart salute. 'How do you like it?'

Abby retrieved the bags of shopping lying forgotten inside her front door and unpacked far enough to find the container of milk.

For a few moments she was nervous, certain that Ben would want to take the time to drink the steaming beverage while he gathered up his energies after a long day, certain that he would use the opportunity to ply her with more questions.

Nothing could have been further from the truth.

'No slacking!' he exclaimed, when he handed her a large pottery mug and she leaned against the work-surface, gingerly cradling it between her hands. 'Drink with one hand and work with the other—you've had plenty of practice at St Augustine's!'

Abby chuckled and threw him a salute of her own, and the next half-hour was spent fielding a stream of nonsense observations about the history of the old converted building she lived in and answering another stream of questions about the hospital and their colleagues there.

'How come you don't know all this?' she demanded through her laughter when she'd finished telling him about the recent spate of weddings in the department and the shenanigans that some of the staff had got up to during the fund-raising auction.

'You've been here for several months now, and everyone always gossips like mad. Or...' A strangely unwelcome thought crossed her mind, and she turned to face him as she continued, 'Perhaps you're one of those who like to keep your social life separate from the hospital and the people working there?' just like the man who'd impersonated him...

'I've never really had time for gossiping, and as for my social life...' He shrugged and Abby's interest was piqued when she became certain that he was avoiding her eyes. To her surprise she saw a faint wash of colour darken his cheek-bones. 'I've always been pretty much of a workaholic so I've never really had much time for that either.'

'But you went out somewhere the other evening—

somewhere formal,' she reminded him, the image of his tie-less evening shirt coming back to haunt her.

His sharp glance at her told her that he was remembering the way that evening had ended, too, and made her wish that she'd kept her mouth shut. She was very surprised when he volunteered an explanation.

'I'd been to the opera with an old friend of my parents'. The tickets were booked a while ago and—'

The shrilling of the phone interrupted him and Abby had to bite back an exclamation of annoyance. How often was she likely to have such an insight into his private life? Heaven knew, she'd always been interested—had actually thought she'd been part of it. And now...

She turned to reach for the noisy instrument, but before she could lift it her forgotten answerphone clicked into action. A quick glance down at the display panel showed that there were already several messages waiting for her and she paused to find out who this latest caller was before she broke in.

'Abby?'

The single word was enough to freeze the blood in her veins and send a shiver of revulsion up her spine, every hair standing to attention.

'Oh, God,' she breathed, her eyes flying towards the kitchen just in time to see Ben appear in the doorway.

'Who is it?' he demanded softly, responding to the distress on her face.

'Abby?' the voice said again stridently. 'Abby, pick up the phone. I know you're there—I've been watching and I saw the lights come on,' he continued ominously.

There was a pause then the sound of a vicious muttered curse before the connection was broken.

Abby's hand was still suspended in mid-air over the telephone when the call ended, and she stared at it as the tremor in her fingers grew visibly worse.

'Who was that?'

Ben's deep voice drew her attention out of the pit of dread into which she'd been sinking, and she was surprised into a wry chuckle.

'Surprisingly enough, until just a few days ago I thought it was you.'

'What?'

The look on his face would have been funny if it hadn't been for the topic of conversation.

'*That* was the person who's been calling himself Ben Taylor,' she said succinctly.

'But he doesn't sound anything *like* me,' he objected after a startled pause.

'Not then he didn't,' she agreed. 'I can only assume that when he was with me he must have changed his accent to match yours. It must have slipped his control when he got angry.'

'Well, one thing that's proved,' Ben pointed out grimly. 'At least you now know for certain that it wasn't me. I couldn't have been telephoning you if I'm standing here, listening to the call.'

'I'd already decided that it couldn't have been you,' Abby said softly, deeply affected by the chaotic mix of pain and anger she saw him trying to hide. 'The person I've been working with these last few months is far too trustworthy to do such a thing.'

It was some while before Abby was able to persuade Ben that the locks on her windows and doors were proof against even the most determined intruder. At last she was able to persuade him that he'd done enough for her and she was able to close the door behind him.

She didn't doubt that he would have been willing to stay and keep her company if she'd admitted to the fear that swept through her whenever she allowed herself two seconds to think about it.

In spite of the nightmare events of the last few days, she was still attracted to the man and would have enjoyed spending time with him, but suddenly she'd felt the need to be alone.

Too many things were happening at once, and if she was going to be able to cope with her demanding job she needed to get her head organised. The last thing she needed was the distraction Ben would provide as she tried to get her flat back to order. She needed to feel that she was taking control again, and that wasn't going to happen while he was there.

It was bad enough finding her eyes drawn towards him as they worked together at St Augustine's, but trying to catch another glimpse of his lean, hair-sprinkled stomach as he reached up to wash the fingerprint powder from her paintwork was more than her frazzled nerves could stand.

Unfortunately, out of sight didn't mean out of mind, and when she finally went to sleep it wasn't long before her nightmares took on a new twist, with an ever-increasing number of replicas of Ben tormenting her from every direction.

By day she felt that she was managing to function fairly efficiently, but as time went by her lack of restful sleep began to take its toll.

'Sister, could I have a word with you, please?' Big Mac said one afternoon in what sounded like the terrifyingly quiet voice she usually reserved for reprimands.

Abby meekly trailed after her superior towards her office, not in the least surprised that the older woman didn't need to look to make sure she was following. It wouldn't occur to any of the nurses under her to refuse such a request.

'Sit down, Abby, please,' she invited, indicating one of the chairs in front of her desk. Abby complied, resigned to the fact that any reprimand was probably warranted—she really wasn't working as well as she should.

Instead of positioning herself behind her desk, as Abby had expected, the older woman sat in the chair next to her.

'Now, dear, I thought it was time we had a little review of the situation,' she began in her softly precise Scots accent. 'It's nearly three weeks now since your…accident, and as far as I can see you still aren't looking very well. You've lost weight and you look as white as a ghost, and I can't remember the last time I heard you laugh.'

The kindly expression on her superior's face was almost the last straw, and Abby had to fight hard to contain the tears that welled perilously close to the surface.

'Would it help if you had some time off, my dear? It would give you a chance to catch up on your sleep at least and, as for the rest, I could recommend someone—'

'Oh, no, Sister!' The thought of spending any more time in her flat was horrible. Every corner seemed to harbour grim memories, and if that wasn't enough she'd been reduced to spending her evenings almost without light because as soon as she switched one on the phone would ring.

It seemed as if she just couldn't win. When she was awake she had the permanent feeling that someone was watching her, and when she tried to sleep the demons she repressed when she was awake were released to torment her anew.

'Please, Sister, I'd rather be at work—I'd rather be busy than sitting around twiddling my thumbs. I've never been very good at that.'

'That's all very well, Abby, and I can understand you looking on your work as a lifeline, but my responsibility is also to the patients. So far there hasn't been a problem, but how much longer do you think I can let it go on before I'm putting patients at risk because you're too exhausted to concentrate?'

'I'm sorry, Sister.' Abby fixed her gaze on her white knuckles, her fingers tightly laced together as guilt seemed to slide a sharp knife between her ribs. 'If you think my work is unsatisfactory...'

'It's not *that* so much as being worried about you, my dear.' She reached across to pat the knotted hands, and part of Abby's mind registered that her touch felt very warm in comparison with her own chilly fingers. 'You're an excellent nurse and I'd hate to lose you, but if you don't manage to find some way to get yourself back on an even keel I'm afraid you're going to burn out.'

Abby knew she was right, but before she could find the words to reply there was a tap at the door.

'It's only an hour to the end of your shift,' Celia MacDonald said as she shot spryly to her feet. 'I suggest you go home early and have a good think about what you want to do. This is my home number so if you feel you need to talk to me away from the hospital I'm only too willing.'

She passed Abby a piece of paper and captured her hand for a moment. 'Obviously, because of confidentiality I've never been told exactly what happened that night, but I have my suspicions. I would hate for you to survive one trauma only to lose the profession you love because of the after-effects.'

The knock at the door was repeated as Abby forced out her husky thanks, immeasurably moved by her superior's empathy.

She clambered clumsily to her feet as the senior sister went to open the door, feeling utterly weary.

'Hello, Doctor. Come in. Come in. And what can I do for you?' the older woman said briskly, and Abby could hear the smile in her voice.

'I was looking for one of your nurses,' said a familiar voice. 'Someone said they saw her following you in this direction.'

Abby turned sharply to find herself almost face to face with a frowning Ben Taylor.

Suddenly it felt as if all her blood was draining down towards her feet and she could feel herself swaying, her head hardly connected to her body at all.

CHAPTER FOUR

'CATCH her...'

'Oh, my dear...'

Voices spiralled around Abby as her knees suddenly refused to bear her weight, but before she could hit the floor she was caught up in a pair of strong arms and deposited unceremoniously back into the chair she'd just vacated.

'Keep your head down,' Ben ordered gruffly, one hand resting firmly on her shoulder. 'Give yourself a chance to recover.'

'I'm sorry,' Abby muttered, mortified, her voice muffled by its close proximity to her lap. All she could think was that at least he hadn't dumped her in the recovery position on the floor. 'I must have got up too quickly.'

Everything was still whirling around so she kept her eyes tightly closed, but that only seemed to make her more aware of the warmth of Ben's hand on her shoulder and the indefinable mixture of soap and man that was his signature—even with her eyes closed.

'My dear soul, what on earth brought that on?' exclaimed Celia MacDonald somewhere in the background. 'You're not on one of these faddy diets, are you?'

'I hope not,' Ben commented grimly, as his hand tightened briefly over her shoulder. 'When did you last eat, woman? You're nothing but skin and bones.'

Abby drew a deep, steadying breath and slowly sat

up, but she still felt very vulnerable now that Ben had also straightened up and was looming over her. She had to look such a very long way before she reached his frowning face.

'Of course I'm not dieting,' she snapped. 'I keep far too busy for weight to catch up with me.' She couldn't help feeling a little guilty as she refuted his accusation. If she was strictly honest, she hadn't really felt much like eating since she was attacked, and recently just the thought of food was enough to make her feel green.

'Well, something's not right. You look dreadful, and it's been going on long enough,' he retorted belligerently. 'I think we ought to run a few tests just to make certain that you didn't suffer any damage that wasn't picked up at the time.'

'Damage? What sort of damage?' Abby demanded. 'All the bruising completely disappeared weeks ago.'

'Abby, dear, I think he's right,' Celia interrupted quietly. 'If there was any internal damage—for example, to your kidneys—surely it would be worth it to set everyone's mind at rest?'

Abby tried to give in graciously, but she was torn two ways. Part of her was fighting the idea that she was suffering any after-effects of that night, but the other part was secretly glad that she was being allowed no option. With these two civilised bulldozers behind her she could guarantee that if there was anything wrong with her, robbing her of her energy and appetite, the tests they would put her through would find it.

She had to fight a smile when Ben tried to lead her off to perform the tests, apparently intending to take the samples himself.

'Go on with you, Doctor,' Celia MacDonald chided, flapping a dismissive hand at him. 'You've got other things to do and I think you can quite safely leave this to the two of us now.'

Abby knew that, as a non-urgent patient, some of the tests would have to wait their turn and it would be several days before she knew the results.

It was the findings of one of the simpler tests that shocked her most, and the senior sister had just broken the news to her when Ben reappeared on the scene. She felt almost as if she were sleepwalking as he took her by the arm and escorted her out of the department.

In spite of her disorientation, she was vaguely aware that Celia MacDonald had handed him her jacket and bag, and then he was leading her swiftly out of the department before they could encounter any inquisitive colleagues.

It wasn't until he'd unlocked his car and tried to usher her into the passenger seat that she began to snap out of her stupor.

'What are you doing?' she asked, balking at climbing into the glove-soft leather seat, no matter how inviting it looked. 'I brought my own car in this morning.'

That fact alone was enough to put a frown on her face.

Once upon a time she'd enjoyed the brisk walk to work, but ever since that night she'd felt as if there were eyes watching her wherever she went. She'd found that at least there was an illusion of safety when she had her 'tin overcoat' around her.

'You're in no fit state to drive,' he pointed out gently, and gave her a nudge.

Abby's shaky legs forced her to confess that he was right so she gave in without any further fight.

As she watched him circle the car with his familiar easy stride she had to admit that in spite of the devastating news she'd just received there was something very reassuring about being in Ben's presence.

Almost against her will she'd found herself watching him over the last few weeks, and she'd realised that he was every bit as confident and dependable as she'd first thought. In fact, the more she thought about it the more she wondered how any impostor could have fooled her, no matter how well rehearsed.

He started the engine and soothing music began to pour out softly around her, the car filled with the skilful sound of an expertly played classical guitar.

Abby smiled when she recognised the track as one in her own collection of CDs and began to relax.

'Abby, can I ask you something?'

She blinked at the question, suddenly realising that although he'd started the engine he was gazing out of the windscreen with his hands linked on top of the steering-wheel.

'What?' Her pulse suddenly started to gallop when she realised that he must know the results of the tests too, and she braced herself, certain that he was going to mention it.

'Are you still getting those phone calls?'

The question was so unexpected that it took a moment for her to set her mind off in a new direction.

'Tell me to mind my own business, if you'd rather, but—'

'No... I mean yes,' she stammered, then had to begin again. 'No, I don't mind. After all, you were there when he phoned that time and, yes, he's still leaving messages—when I plug the machine in.'

'What do you mean?' His forehead was creased with a concerned frown.

'It's been getting to me,' she said quietly, staring down at her knotted fingers and hating having to admit to a feeling of vulnerability. 'Sometimes the phone will go all evening, and then I disconnect it to get some peace.' She couldn't help glancing across at him and was heartened by the compassion in his gaze. 'The trouble is, I feel I have to plug it back in before I go to work, and by the time I get home again he's filled the tape.'

'So that's why you've been looking so exhausted, and that was *before* the latest...' He didn't complete the sentence, and Abby was relieved when he subsided into silence for a moment, a thoughtful expression on his face as he seemed to look straight through her.

'Do you want an evening off?' he demanded suddenly.

'Pardon?' She wasn't certain what he was suggesting.

'To borrow a cliché, let me take you away from all this. I can't offer tropical isles or a life of unimaginable luxury, but I can offer an evening of peace and quiet and a meal you don't have to cook for yourself.'

Abby could feel the smile creeping over her face in answer to his nonsense. A few minutes ago, she hadn't thought she'd feel like smiling for the next hundred years or so.

She needed to do some serious thinking but she'd been dreading the prospect of trying to do it in the claustrophobic confines of her flat—especially knowing that she was going to have to disconnect the phone if it wasn't to drive her insane.

Suddenly the breathing space of an evening in Ben's company sounded like just what the doctor ordered, and much to her surprise she found herself accepting.

'We could go out somewhere, if you'd feel happier, but I thought…a quiet meal at my place would be more restful…' The tone of uncertainty in his voice touched her deeply. It was such a rare thing to hear it coming from him. In fact, she didn't think she'd ever heard him utter a tentative word when they'd worked together.

Now he seemed almost like a shy young man, asking a girl out on a first date, and it seemed so incongruous, especially in a man accustomed to evenings out at sophisticated venues such as the opera.

A flash of intuition told her why he was being so careful to offer her the choice of locations, and she impulsively turned and rushed into speech.

'I'd far rather spend a quiet evening with you,' she admitted emotionally, grateful for his sensitivity to her feelings. 'I'm not really in the mood to be surrounded by strangers.' Apart from the fact that every time she went anywhere she had a crawling sensation over her skin as if she was being watched… 'Anyway,' she added hurriedly, eager to reassure him, 'I know you're a trustworthy man.'

Her words hung in the sudden silence stretching between them and Abby realised, too late, how they must have sounded to him.

Embarrassment brought her thought processes to a standstill and she bit her lips as she felt the scorching heat of a blush creep up her throat and into her cheeks. If only she'd bitten her tongue sooner, she thought.

What on earth must the man think of her, gushing at him like that?

'Thank you,' he said softly, and a slightly husky tone had crept into his voice. 'That's the nicest thing you could have said to me, especially in view of...' He gestured in lieu of completing the thought and turned to set the car in motion as he continued. 'I *was* wondering if it was too soon, if you'd be too wary to trust anyone yet.'

'Perhaps that's part of my problem,' she suggested with a wry smile, relaxing into the comfort of her seat and taking the brake off her tongue again now that she knew he understood. 'I got to know you a bit through working with you at the hospital so when...whoever-he-was asked me out I transferred the trust *you'd* earned to him. Unfortunately...'

'So, if you look at it that way, it's partly my fault that it happened to you,' he said, shocking her into a gasp.

'No way!' she exclaimed heatedly. 'How *could* it be?'

'Well, if I hadn't been such a sterling sort of chap—such a paragon of all the manly virtues—you'd probably have been far more wary of him,' he offered, and his impossibly smug delivery made her laugh aloud for the first time in weeks.

'Idiot,' she choked, and realised that although nothing had really changed, his nonsense had made her feel much better about herself.

She knew she still had some tough decisions to make, but with Ben Taylor's steady presence beside her for some reason they no longer seemed so insurmountable.

* * *

'How about an omelette?' Ben's voice sounded muffled as it emerged from behind the open fridge door. 'I can offer alternative fillings of...' there was the sound of shuffling '...cheese, cheese and tomato, bacon, bacon and tomato or mushroom.'

He emerged with a small plastic bag held triumphantly aloft then frowned as he took a closer look at the contents.

'On second thoughts delete mushrooms from the list. These look as if they can't decide whether to fight back or ask for a decent burial.'

'Cheese and tomato sounds perfect,' she assured him through another chuckle as she settled herself more comfortably on the kitchen stool he'd pulled out for her.

It seemed as if he'd deliberately set out to entertain her, right from that first startled bout of laughter in his car.

She hadn't realised, in the often life-and-death surroundings of the A and E department, that under his professional white coat was a very humorous man. She couldn't remember him joining in some of the sessions of gallows humour so prevalent in hospitals.

Well, she was certainly getting to see this other side of him now.

It had started with the cautious way he'd opened his front door. At first she'd thought he was being careful not to let a pet escape...until he'd turned to her and demanded in a stage whisper, 'Can you hear them?'

'Hear who?'

She strained her ears, but the house seemed silent. The only sounds were the distant hum of traffic on the main road several hundred yards away and the early summer evening cheeps and rustles of birds settling down in the trees.

'Not *who*—what?' he clarified, his expression very serious. 'Do you think they'll let us in?'

'What?'

What on earth was he talking about?

'My socks,' he said impatiently, finally pushing the door open as if the answer should have been obvious. 'Every time I wash a load some of them escape, never to be seen again. I think they've all gone into hiding while they plan world domination.'

He'd pretended to be wounded by her laughter but he couldn't hide the gleam in his eyes.

His quick guided tour of the house whetted her appetite for decorating, especially when he kept apologising for the rather spartan appearance of the place. The only really expensive item she saw was a state-of-the-art sound system with an extensive selection of CDs. He held up a couple of them to offer her the choice, and she pointed to another one of Spanish guitar music.

'I'm not certain yet quite what style to go for,' Ben continued, as he smiled and nodded at her selection and turned to insert it. 'I've only lived in hospital accommodation or rented flats before, and there's never really been the incentive to do much more than keep it clean. This time...' He shrugged and glanced round at the plain white walls.

'It all looks rather...clinical,' Abby offered hesitantly, noting the total absence of any softening touches like cushions and pictures. Even the windows had blinds rather than curtains.

'Is that the result of too many hours in a clinical atmosphere, do you think? Perhaps I need a complete change. What do you think of Gothic—all dark and shadowy and mysterious?'

The banter continued through the meal and Abby insisted on sharing cleaning duties when they'd finished.

'That was the best meal I've had in ages,' she said sincerely as she sat down with a steaming mug of coffee to enjoy the latest selection of Chopin piano preludes. 'You're a far better cook than I am.'

'Unfortunately, my repertoire is rather limited, but while I was training it was a case of learning to fend for myself or starving.'

'I'm sure over the years there were plenty of women willing to see if the way to your heart was through your stomach,' she teased, and was surprised to see his flush of embarrassment.

'Not really.' There was a touching vulnerability in the way he avoided meeting her eyes. 'I've always been rather focused on my work, rather than pubbing and clubbing and going to discos.'

'Ah!' She wagged a finger at him, still somewhat amazed at how relaxed she felt in his company. It was almost as if she'd known him for years. 'You know what they say. All work and no play…'

He was silent for a moment.

'Do you think I'm dull, Abby?' he asked, his hazel eyes watching her intently while he waited for her reply, almost as if the answer really mattered to him.

'Far from it,' she answered honestly, knowing she'd been attracted to him from the first time she'd seen him. She'd obviously appreciated his brand of dark good looks, as had the rest of the female staff in the department and beyond, but for the first time in her life she'd believed there'd been something more to it than that.

The attraction had only deepened over the ensuing months as she'd learned how good a doctor he was and how compassionate a man.

One thing she'd never had a chance to find out before tonight was how much she would enjoy his exclusive company and how much she was beginning to dread her return home.

The thought of home reminded her suddenly that she still had some heavy-duty thinking to do. She'd been enjoying herself so much that time had simply ceased to have any meaning.

'In fact, I can't remember an evening when I've laughed more, but I mustn't outstay my welcome. We've both got to be up in the morning and by the time you've taken me home...'

For a moment she thought he was going to say something but he gave a nod of acquiescence and went to get his keys, detouring briefly to switch off the music.

'I can't thank you enough,' she murmured as he drew to a halt outside her front door a short time later. 'I hadn't realised how much my brain needed the light relief... And my stomach thanks you too.'

'They're more than welcome,' he said with a smile. 'Perhaps you'll bring them round again some time.'

With his own innate brand of courtesy he insisted on escorting her the few paces to her front door, and she'd just looked up at him to repeat her thanks when he drew her to a halt.

Her heart rate speeded up and deep inside she felt a sharp twist of awareness that he might be intending to end their evening with a kiss.

'Are you sure you locked your door?' he demanded suddenly, and she realised that there was nothing remotely romantic in the expression on his face.

His forehead was pleated and his brows were drawn into a deep frown. The tension radiating off him told her that there was something seriously wrong.

'Of course. Why?' She glanced towards her front door and saw what had caught his eye. 'Oh, my God,' she breathed, and took a step forward, her own eyes widening when she saw the damage around the lock and the way it was standing partly open.

'Here.' He grabbed her arm and pulled her back, handing her his keys. 'Get in the car and lock the doors.'

'Why?' She couldn't believe what she was seeing and his words weren't making any sense.

'Abby, whoever did this could still be in there,' he said patiently, then turned her back towards the car and gave her a gentle push. 'I need to know you're safe before I go in there.'

'But if he's still in there, *you* could get hurt,' she pointed out, surprised by how much the thought worried her.

'There aren't many people who'd tangle with me,' he said, stating nothing more than the obvious. 'Anyway, rather me than you.'

Abby would have liked to argue with him but she now felt she knew him well enough to know that there was no way she could win.

She watched anxiously from the security of his car while he pushed the door open and disappeared inside. He seemed to be gone for a very long time.

There were no sounds of violence from within or she'd have become worried enough to defy him and follow him inside by the time the light came on at her sitting-room window and Ben reappeared at the front door.

'What is it? What's happened?' she demanded as she tumbled out of the car on shaky legs and joined him on her front path.

'Someone's broken in and done some damage,' he said succinctly, and she could see from the set of his jaw that he was suppressing some strong emotions.

'Damage? What sort of damage?' She stepped around him and started to make for her front door.

'Abby...' He caught her arm and drew her to a halt. 'I've phoned the police and they said not to touch anything.'

'OK. So I won't touch anything,' she agreed belligerently. 'But it's my flat and I need to see what's happened. It can't be worse than what my imagination's coming up with.'

He released his hold on her and followed her into her little hallway. It wasn't until she stood in the entrance of her sitting room that she realised that sometimes reality was far worse than imagination.

At her gasp of dismay his arm came around her shoulders, and as she surveyed the devastation it tightened to hold her more closely against his strength.

'Everything,' she whispered when she'd visually catalogued the curtains slashed to ribbons and the upholstery disembowelled across the sodden carpet. 'It's all been destroyed.'

In spite of his support she swayed as shock took the starch out of her knees. The light caught on shards of glass where every one of her pictures and photographs had been shattered beyond recognition.

'Why?' She looked up at him and when she read

the expression on his face she knew her own must have been displaying her utter disbelief.

A car drew up outside the house, the sound travelling to them clearly through the open front door.

'Abby? Are you there?' called a voice, and Ben pivoted so that they faced the doorway in time for WPC Cassidy to appear, closely followed by DC Sharp.

'You discovered this, sir?' DC Sharp asked, his eyebrow raised when he saw the way Ben was holding Abby close beside him.

There was something in the way he was looking at them or the way he asked the question that Ben didn't like because Abby felt the sudden tension in his body.

'Yes. I phoned in as soon as I saw what had happened and asked the person on the switchboard to notify you. Thank you for coming so quickly.'

'And was Miss Walker in the house when it happened?' the officer continued, totally ignoring Ben's thanks. 'Or was she with you when you discovered it?'

'*She* can speak for herself,' Abby pointed out, her anger at the way DC Sharp was treating Ben suddenly restoring her backbone. He hadn't deserved her accusation three weeks ago and certainly wasn't responsible for this outrage. She glared at the policeman as she continued.

'I returned home about…' She glanced at her watch and was amazed to see how much time had passed since they'd drawn up outside her flat. 'About twenty or thirty minutes ago. Dr Taylor drove me here after we'd had supper together. He hasn't been out of my sight for any longer than the time it takes to visit the bathroom since we both left the hospital together at the end of our shift late this afternoon. So if you're thinking of trying to pin this on him—don't.'

A slight cough drew her eyes to Beth Cassidy and she saw that the young woman's eyes were gleaming with repressed laughter at her superior's dressing-down.

'Yes, well, then,' DC Sharp mumbled, and glanced around the room. 'I presume you had a look round to see if the flat was empty. Is this the lot or have any other rooms been trashed?'

'I'm afraid it's the whole flat,' Ben said. His arm tightened around Abby once again when she made a wordless sound of dismay, then he continued, 'The bedroom's the worst. There's graffiti in there too.'

DC Sharp raised a questioning eyebrow then turned to make his way along the short corridor.

He was gone for several minutes and when he returned there was a look of disgust on his usually well-controlled face.

'The scene-of-crime officer will probably be along soon to see what evidence they can pick up, but you're not going to be able to stay here. Is there anywhere you could go? A colleague you could stay with?'

'Oh, but...' Abby paused to make some rapid mental calculations. Her bank balance wouldn't stand many more nights in alternative accommodation, no matter how welcoming Mrs Halloran was. Unfortunately, it was obvious from the state of the place and the fact that she'd never be able to secure the front door that she couldn't sleep here tonight.

Even if she *could* lock the door she doubted that she'd dare let herself fall asleep. The systematic devastation all around her was proof that whoever had done this had an evil temper, and for some reason he seemed to have decided to vent it on her.

'She can stay with me,' Ben said decisively, taking a card out of his wallet and handing it to the officer. 'I know you've got it on file but that's the address. It's had quite a lot of work done on it recently, including new security locks on doors and windows and an infrared camera, so she'll be quite safe.'

'Well, you might as well take her away, sir. There's obviously not much she can do here until the SOCO's been and done his job in case there *are* any fingerprints. We'll arrange for the property to be properly secured before we leave and then she can come in tomorrow and make a list of anything that's gone missing.'

'As if I'm going to be able to tell,' Abby said dryly, with a pointed glance around her. 'Is it all right if I go into the bathroom to get my wash kit and the bedroom for a change of clothes? I'll be careful not to touch anything else.'

There was an ominous silence that no one seemed anxious to fill, and she glanced from one to the other.

'Actually…'

'That probably won't be…'

'Abby, I can lend you anything…'

Suddenly the three of them had hurried into speech and she knew there was something badly wrong.

'What is it?' she demanded. 'Ben, what aren't you telling me?' She tried to loosen his hold on her but he wouldn't allow it.

'Abby…'

'No, Ben. Dammit, don't try to hide things from me. I'm stronger than I look. Ask Beth.' She indicated the young WPC hovering in the hallway. 'She's the liaison officer who was assigned to me after I was...after I was attacked.'

'It's not that I doubt your determination, Abby,' he said soothingly. 'I wouldn't dare. It's just that there honestly isn't any point in your trying to salvage anything from either your bathroom or bedroom.'

'Nothing?' she whispered, her voice suddenly shaky in spite of her brave words when she thought of the pretty things she'd begun to collect once she'd qualified. 'There's nothing left at all?'

'Anything that wasn't ripped up was sprayed with paint or doused with bleach,' he explained, meeting her eyes so that she could judge his honesty.

With a cry of distress she whirled away from him and stumbled towards the other half of her flat, suddenly needing to see for herself that there was truly nothing left—that all she had in the world was what she stood up in.

'Oh, my God,' she breathed in shock, and staggered back a pace, grateful that Ben had followed her or she might have fallen.

He'd said that the bedroom was worse than the sitting room and she'd thought she'd known what to expect, but never in her life would she have imagined that anyone would have added to the horror of the scene by spray-painting such vile obscenities across her walls.

She heard a whimpering sound, almost like an animal in pain, but it wasn't until she heard Ben trying to quieten her that she realised *she* was the one making the noise.

'Come on, Abby. Let's get you out of here,' he said, and began to guide her away from the scene.

She rallied when he joined her in the car and tried

to persuade him to take her to the little bed-and-breakfast she'd stayed at before, but he wasn't having any of it.

'Be sensible, Abby,' he said quietly, and turned the car in the opposite direction, setting a course for his own house.

'Sensible?' she repeated, and heard the shrill edge to her voice. 'Why is going back to your place any more sensible than going to Mrs Halloran's? I'll be perfectly all right.'

'And if he's following you and decides to break in during the night? How safe would you be then?'

His calm logic stopped her in her tracks.

In all conscience she couldn't run the risk that whoever he was would destroy Mrs Halloran's house the way he had hers.

'Anyway,' Ben continued sombrely as he drew to a halt in his driveway, 'there's more to consider than just your own safety—unless you've already decided to get rid of the baby.'

CHAPTER FIVE

THE baby.

Abby felt the blood drain out of her face again the way it had when Celia MacDonald had given her the news.

Her hand crept across to lie over her flat stomach. She couldn't believe the enormity of the changes that had happened in her life in the last few weeks, but she was afraid they were nothing compared to the changes that were still to come.

A baby, she thought with a measure of despair. A baby to carry and give birth to and bring up in the world without the help of a loving father. The prospect was more than daunting.

A quiet voice at the back of her mind tried to tempt her with the possibility that she could turn back the clock—could have her old life back if she were to do what Ben seemed to be accusing her of deciding.

'No!' Abby gasped, as everything inside her revolted at the idea.

'No, you're not worried about your safety or, no, you haven't made a decision about the baby?' he demanded, his tone far too belligerent for someone just standing on the sidelines of her life.

'I haven't made any decisions about anything,' she retorted fiercely. 'And I don't like other people making decisions *for* me either.'

'It's hardly an earth-shattering thing to offer you a bed for the night when you've nowhere better to go,' he pointed out with an irritating return to cool logic. 'Would you rather we sat here in the car while you make a list of your alternatives?'

Abby couldn't say a word, silent in the face of his unexpected sarcasm.

'Oh, Abby, I'm sorry,' Ben muttered gruffly into the shrinking space of the car's interior, the tension almost humming between them. 'The last thing you need is more grief, but all I wanted to do was give you somewhere safe to go. After that business with the police it's getting far too late to go wandering about, looking for somewhere.'

While he was speaking he'd turned into his driveway and had halted the car. He released his seat belt and twisted, his knee hitched up across the handbrake and his arm hooked over the back of his seat as he faced her.

'You only need to stay the one night, if that's what you'd prefer,' he said earnestly. 'And I promise you'll be perfectly safe.'

Abby couldn't reply for a moment because her emotions were in such turmoil.

She was very aware that his hand was resting within inches of her shoulder and his knee was almost touching her thigh but his very stillness was a sort of comfort.

Apart from that, she'd spent many hours with him over the last few months, and while she'd once imagined they shared an attraction towards each other he'd never done anything to suggest that he had any lecherous feelings towards her.

Her practical side was telling her to grab his offer with both hands, knowing that his altruism was utterly genuine, but her fear was holding her back as the memories of her last close encounter with a man loomed large.

'You'll be perfectly safe,' he repeated persuasively. 'There's even a brand-new lock on the bedroom door.'

'Oh, Ben,' she exclaimed, his name emerging on a sob born of bewilderment. 'I know you're trustworthy—it's not that. It's…' She gave up and shook her head.

'I know what it is,' he announced decisively as he removed the key from the ignition and opened his door. 'You're tired and scared and confused, and what you need is a long hot shower and a clean, warm bed and about twelve uninterrupted hours of sleep.'

Abby knew he was right. 'Chance would be a fine thing,' she muttered as she gave in and followed him back into his house.

'Make yourself at home,' he said over his shoulder as he leapt two steps at a time up the stairs, his long legs making nothing of the gradient. 'Put the kettle on if you want another drink. I won't be long.'

Abby wandered into the kitchen, but when she got there she realised that she didn't really want anything more.

She leaned shakily against the work surface and found herself idly contemplating the various items attached to the bulletin board over the fridge.

'Dental appointment. Car MOT,' she read, smiling when she saw that one wasn't due for four months and the other one should have taken place more than a month ago. Obviously, once an item reached the board it took up semi-permanent residence there.

She twisted her head to read a hand-written note in his familiar angular scrawl. 'Ring Carolyn re: tickets for opera…'

That wiped the smile off her face.

Who was Carolyn?

'Right!'

Ben's voice behind her nearly made her jump out of her skin. She'd been so wrapped up in her thoughts that she hadn't even heard him come down the stairs.

'I've put clean towels and a spare toothbrush on the side next to the basin, and I've left a couple of offerings of substitute nightwear with them. The water's running and the bathroom's all yours—take your time.'

Her cheeks burning with mortification at being caught snooping into his private life, Abby scurried up the stairs and bolted herself into the bright, airy bathroom.

A blissful half-hour later she emerged, leaving a room filled with steam but with every inch of her body scrubbed clean.

In the absence of any alternative she'd rinsed her underwear and hung it discreetly on the end of the heated towel rail behind the door. The T-shirt Ben had offered her was long enough to cover her essentials, but it still felt strange to be walking about his house without any underwear on.

She knew that the fine cotton shirt had been intended as an alternative to the T-shirt, but when she'd looked down at herself and realised just how much of her was visible through her makeshift nightwear she'd decided to use it as a substitute dressing-gown. It was either that or she would have to appropriate the large towelling one hanging on the back of the door.

She gave it a last longing look. It was much more substantial than the well-worn softness of what she was wearing. It would be all cosy and comfortable and would cover her from her neck to her ankles. It would also surround her with the familiar mixture of soap and man that she would always recognise as Ben.

Unfortunately, she had an idea that this might leave him walking about in nothing more than his underwear, and while she would love to see if his body lived up to the advance billing her imagination had given it she knew her system had undergone enough stress for one day.

'You found everything you needed?' Ben asked, and made her jump again.

'I wish you wouldn't do that,' she complained, as she grabbed for the makeshift turban she'd fashioned around her wet hair with a towel. 'Can't you make a noise to let me know you're there?'

'It's a bit difficult to make a lot of noise on a carpet with bare feet,' he pointed out with a grin, lifting one to show her as he balanced an armful of rumpled bed linen. 'I'll just go and bung this lot in the machine, but in the meantime there are clean sheets on the bed.'

He nodded towards the open door behind him and set off down the stairs, not giving her time to tell him he needn't have bothered going to so much trouble for her. She could have put clean sheets on the spare-room bed herself.

Except it wasn't the spare room she found herself in when she looked around.

'Ben, I can't turn you out of your room,' she protested as she followed him downstairs. 'I can easily use—'

'You're not turning me out. I volunteered,' he pointed out. 'I promised you that your room would have a lock on the door and the only other one in the house is the bathroom.'

'Yes, but—'

'But nothing.' He grabbed her by her shoulders and propelled her towards the stairs. 'You're out on your feet and you need the peace and comfort of a proper bed.'

He was right, Abby admitted as she folded his shirt at the foot of the bed to use in the morning, slid between two layers of crisp fresh cotton and sighed with delight. This *was* what she needed.

Somewhere downstairs she heard the opening notes of a piece of guitar music and smiled.

'Perfect,' she whispered into the shadows of a room lit only by the yellow glow of suburban streetlights.

The notes flowed up towards her in exquisite mimicry of rippling water and soaring birdsong, twining itself around her until she finally relaxed towards sleep.

Her final coherent thought before she surrendered was that she must remember to ask Ben for the name of the composer...

The nightmare burst on her with the force of a hurricane, with images of her ruined belongings coming at her from every direction while unseen hands dragged her into dark realms of pain.

She tried to struggle but the tatters of her shredded clothing seemed to hold her pinioned while her voice emerged as nothing more than a terrified whimper.

'I've got you now, Abby,' said a deep male voice in the darkness, and she redoubled her efforts even though she knew what was going to happen next— what *always* happened next—and that she could do nothing to stop it.

'Abby!'

There was that voice again, closer and more insistent, and his hands were on her shoulders, on her arms. Any moment now they would tighten as he dragged her along the hallway, their grip becoming crueller as she tried desperately to escape the inevitable.

'Come on, Abby. Wake up.'

The voice was sharper but the hands hadn't grown vicious yet... But they would...they always did...

'Abby, sweetheart, you're dreaming. Wake up.'

The voice was growing louder and clearer, but where in the past it had always berated her now it was gentle. His hands were smoothing her tangled hair away from her face so gently that it was almost as if she were in a different dream.

'Abby. Can you hear me?'

'Yes,' she whispered, compelled to speak by the insistence in his tone.

'Abby. Open your eyes,' he demanded. 'Open your eyes and look at me.'

Her eyelids felt as though they were weighted with lead and her whole body tensed with the effort, but she managed to obey the gentle command.

'It's Ben, Abby. Can you see me?' he asked, and Abby turned her head to focus on the figure sitting on the side of the bed.

In the strange yellow half-light she struggled to make out the familiar features as he leaned towards her. Her eyes strained until she finally saw the dark hollows of his eyes, the lean planes of his cheeks and the way his forehead was pleated in concern.

As he straightened again she was momentarily distracted by the way his towelling robe gaped open over his bare chest to reveal the dark shadow of body hair, but even in her confusion she knew there were more immediate concerns.

'Ben?'

This had never been in her nightmare before. There had never been a worried-looking figure sitting beside her, hesitantly stroking her hair away from her tear-wet face.

He waited a moment before he spoke again, almost as if he knew that she needed time to get her bearings.

'How long has this been going on?' he asked quietly, when her breathing had slowed almost to normal.

She closed her eyes as a shudder shook her from head to foot.

'Ever since...since he...' She couldn't make herself say the words. The details were always far too vivid in her mind immediately after one of these episodes.

'What? Every night?' He sounded horrified. 'How often?'

'Only once...because I can never go back to sleep again,' she admitted wryly, defeated by bone-numbing weariness. 'Sometimes I don't seem to get much more than a couple of hours before it wakes me.'

He was silent while he considered that.

'Is it the same every time?' His analytical brain had begun to work.

'*This* time was different,' she admitted in surprise. 'Before it was always...what happened three weeks ago, but this time there were all my things, everything in the flat, all flying around, ruined.'

Another element of the dream surfaced.

'I was trapped,' she recalled. 'Everything had wrapped itself around me so I couldn't escape him.'

She was surprised when Ben's glance dropped towards her as she lay in bed, and he began to chuckle.

'Well, that part's easily explained.' He pointed down at her. 'You must have got the bedclothes all tangled around your legs when you were dreaming. Here, let me help you.'

Strong hands tugged at the sheets as he tried to straighten them into some sort of order. When the muddle suddenly righted itself it was purely accidental that she ended up lying in the middle of his bed with her substitute nightdress twisted up around her waist.

She froze, unable to move for a moment as embarrassment surged through her. Then she realised that he was equally transfixed, his gaze completely riveted on the semi-naked body in front of him.

Slowly his eyes travelled the full length of her, and she was startled to feel a strange tingling all over, almost as if he were physically touching her. For a moment she felt herself begin to revel in the sensation—until the growing heat in his eyes made the memories come crashing back.

'Don't,' she whimpered, and scrabbled with trembling fingers at the tangled cloth wrapped around her in a frantic effort to hide herself from him.

'Shh, Abby, shh,' he soothed, as he flicked the covers over her and stepped back from the bed. 'I'm not coming any closer.'

His tone made her think of the way he sometimes calmed fractious children in the department, and she realised how crazy the whole situation had become.

This was Ben, and she'd trusted him enough to agree to spend the night at his house. What was more, she hadn't even considered needing to lock the door to his room before she'd gone to sleep.

She looked up at him again and the expression in his eyes was so calm and reassuring that she began to think that she'd imagined the heat of desire she'd seen there. Had she transferred her memory of the savage carnality on her attacker's face to Ben's?

'Oh, Ben,' she wailed, as everything suddenly overcame her. 'I'm sorry.'

'Ah, Abby, don't cry.' He sounded almost panic-struck at the prospect. 'What do you want me to do? Shall I go out again and shut the door?'

'No. Don't leave me,' she pleaded, and held her hand out to him. 'Please don't leave me alone. The nights are so long and I seem to have been sitting alone in the dark for weeks, waiting for something awful to happen.'

'Shall I turn the light on? Will that help?' He reached out towards the plain, functional lamp beside the bed but she grabbed at his arm to stop him.

Startled by the unexpected heat of his hair-sprinkled muscularity under her hand, she snatched it back and buried it under the covers.

'No. Don't.' She sniffed. 'My face will be all red and blotchy.'

He chuckled and the sound enfolded her almost like a caress in the quiet darkness of the room. 'I always reckon you know that a woman's going to be all right when she starts thinking about her looks,' he mused, obviously tongue-in-cheek.

'Chauvinist,' she hissed, and snatched gratefully at the shadowy white shape of a handkerchief he held out towards her.

As she blew vigorously she had to admit that the tension that seemed to stalk her, night and day, seemed to have diminished just a little.

A long silence stretched out between them, but it

didn't feel awkward until Ben cleared his throat and took a step back.

'Look, it would probably be best if I leave you to try to go back to sleep,' he muttered, and turned towards the door, sure-footed in spite of the darkness.

'No!'

Panic made the single word explode out of her as the terrors swooped towards her again.

'Please, Ben, don't go.'

This time the silence was full of electricity and she could feel him looking at her, gauging the meaning behind her words.

'I told you, I've never been able to get back to sleep after one of these...episodes,' she explained, her cheeks flaming as she rushed into speech when she realised he might have misunderstood. 'It's as if every time I close my eyes it's *there*, all around me.'

He came back so that he was standing beside her again.

'So what do you want me to do? Stay here and talk with you?'

There was wariness in his voice—or was it just tiredness? The fact that he was due at work in the morning made her realise suddenly how selfish she was being.

'You don't have to talk, just...' She shrugged uncomfortably. What exactly *did* she want him to do?

'How about this? I'll sit down on the edge of the bed, and if we talk we talk and if you fall asleep—'

'But that's not fair to you,' she said with an attempt at honesty, even though everything in her was shrieking to accept his offer.

'OK,' he agreed easily, and her heart sank. 'In that

case, I'll lie down beside you and the last one to fall asleep is a rotten egg.'

Abby's insides tangled in a mixture of excitement and fear, but before she could find the words to voice either emotion he'd flopped down beside her.

The springs gave a squeak of protest and then grew silent. The only thing she could hear was the loud thumping of her heart as she fought a battle with her fear.

Her muscles were rigid with tension as she waited for him to speak, to move, to...anything.

He just lay there, still and silent, and when she realised that he wasn't going to make any sudden moves she finally allowed herself to relax.

'OK?' he murmured from just inches away, and she realised that he must have been waiting for her to release the deep breath she'd been holding.

He still hadn't moved but she found she had to force herself to ignore the waves of warmth she could feel radiating towards her from his very large, very male body and concentrate on making her vocal cords work.

'Um...OK,' she agreed, and swallowed hard, all too aware of just how big and how virile he was.

'Am I taking up too much room?' he asked solicitously, his tone garden-party polite.

'Um...no.'

She heard a hastily muffled snort.

'Not very good at scintillating conversation, are we?' he said, and his laughter escaped in a deep chuckle.

Suddenly she was chuckling too, and the tension was broken.

They spoke idly for a while about nothing in particular. Abby hadn't realised she'd actually relaxed enough to fall asleep until the nightmare began to claw at her again.

This time, though, everything was different. This time there were formless, soothing words to prevent the images growing too distinct, warm, strong arms wrapped around her that kept the terror at bay and a deep, rhythmic sound in her ear that drowned the remembered sounds of her attacker's vicious curses and her own terrified screams.

'Abby,' Ben mouthed silently as he looked down at the woman he finally held cradled against his chest. He had to grit his teeth to prevent a string of curses escaping.

Emotionally, he'd always thought she was a remarkably strong woman, her quick mind and ready intelligence evident in everything she did.

Although she was nearly a head shorter than his own six feet plus, he'd never thought of her as being fragile until... He gritted his teeth tighter and wondered fleetingly how much pressure they could take before they shattered.

He'd thought of her as an indomitable woman until she'd stepped out from behind that group of policemen and solicitors in that dingy room and he'd seen her poor, battered face.

He looked down at her lamplit features and was grateful that she'd suffered no permanent scars. His fingers itched to stroke her skin but he didn't want to wake her. She was obviously very close to the edge of exhaustion and needed all the sleep she could get.

He tried to content himself with smoothing his palm over the silky strands of her hair, untangling them from the much darker pelt on his chest with a pang of longing.

How many weeks had he tormented himself with images of those same pale strands spread out across his pillow? But these were hardly the circumstances he'd imagined.

He'd been able to see that she was struggling to cope with the memories and their legacy of fear, and had longed to be able to do something to help.

Each time he'd worked with her in the busy chaos of the accident and emergency department he'd savoured the experience and, in the hope of bolstering her dented self-esteem, had been glad to offer her words of encouragement and appreciation.

Take this afternoon, for example.

A young woman had been brought in by ambulance, obviously badly shaken and almost incoherent after losing an argument with a car on a pedestrian crossing.

Her slurred speech and waving arms had led to the tentative diagnosis that she was either drunk or on drugs and had simply stepped out without warning.

It had been Abby who'd suddenly clapped her hands for attention then pointed to herself and made shapes with her fingers, while saying. 'My name is Abby.'

The beam of relief on their young patient's face made them all realise suddenly that the poor woman was neither drunk nor drugged but deaf.

'Slow down! Slow down!' Abby had laughed when the scraped and bruised fingers had flown into a series of fluid movements as she tried to communicate. 'I only know the signing alphabet so you'll have to spell everything out for me.'

It had been slow and laborious, but with Abby's usual patience it hadn't been long before they'd been able to contact Olivia's friend to come and act as interpreter.

There had been no condescension in his words when, afterwards, he'd praised her for her skill and asked her how she'd acquired it.

'There was a young boy on the children's ward when I was training. He was making his deafness an excuse for not taking his medicine, by pretending he couldn't understand us. I got his mother to teach me a couple of signs and he took over and insisted I learned the whole alphabet so he could "talk" to someone.'

Ben gave a silent snort when he remembered the stupid glow of pride he'd felt when he'd heard the story. As if her kind-heartedness had anything to do with him.

Abby stirred in his arms and drew his attention back to the present moment. His gaze travelled over her with guilty pleasure as he took in the womanly swells and hollows of a body barely concealed under the intimacy of his T-shirt and came to rest on the threatened slenderness of her waist and stomach.

What was she going to decide to do about the unwanted pregnancy the rape had forced on her?

Part of him was revolted at the idea that she would have to bear such a child, knowing that the violence of its conception would forever be at the back of her mind whenever she saw it.

The alternative was even more disturbing and complex, but he didn't think that Abby was the sort of woman who could seek an abortion, even of such a child as this.

There must be something he could do to help her,

he thought, and tightened his arms around her briefly before the heavy oblivion of sleep finally took him.

The sound of early summer birdsong was drifting through the brightening daylight when Abby next opened her eyes and found she had no idea where she was.

For a moment disorientation pleated her forehead then fear stiffened every sinew when she realised that something or someone was pinioning her so that she was unable to move.

Her heart began to pound and she'd drawn in a shaky breath to scream before she remembered the events of the previous night.

'Ben,' she breathed shakily, and all the tension went, leaving her boneless and shaking.

The last thing she remembered was the two of them lying on opposite sides of his bed with a definite no-go area between them.

Now she was plastered against him as closely as a Siamese twin, her head pillowed on his broad chest while his strong arms held her at his side as though she were a precious treasure he didn't want to lose.

She tilted her head slowly until she could look up at him, and saw the dark crescents of his thick lashes fanned out with the innocence of a sleeping child. There was little innocence in the rest of his face, the individual elements of high cheekbones and determined jaw combined with an elegant nose and enticing mouth to make a devilishly handsome whole.

If the nerve endings that were sending back signals from every place where the two of them touched were to be believed, there was nothing wrong with the rest of his body either.

His shoulders were every bit as broad and the darkly furred chest every bit as impressive as she'd imagined.

'Good morning,' Ben said, his husky voice as much a rumble through the wall of that impressive chest as a husky greeting stirring the tendrils of hair against her sleep-warmed cheek.

Her eyes flew up to meet the glint of amusement in his, and she felt that heat double. Had he been watching her while she'd been looking at his body?

'Did you sleep well?' he asked politely when she hid her eyes under half-closed lids. This time she was certain that he was laughing at her.

'Very well, thank you,' she answered primly, and tried to extricate herself from the intimacy of their unintentional embrace.

It must be unintentional, she rationalised, knowing how terrified she'd become in the last weeks about any man coming too close. What if he thought that she'd deliberately wrapped herself around him?

'Good,' he said simply. 'You needed it.' And with the minimum of fuss and effort he slid out of the bed and retrieved his dressing-gown.

Abby caught a flash of dark blue underpants before they were safely covered, but before she could look away from her perusal of the taut muscles that made up his bottom and thighs he'd turned and caught her looking.

'Well, Abby, I didn't think you were the sort of woman to peep!' he teased. 'I'll have the bathroom first this morning,' he continued, not leaving her enough time to protest her innocence, 'then you can have it while I make breakfast. What would you like? Cereal? Toast and coffee?'

It took an effort to banish the mental image of the

perfect symmetry of his nearly naked body from her thoughts, but she managed it.

'Toast, please, and a very large mug of black—' The mental image of her usual wake-up mug of coffee was enough to send her stomach into unexpected instant revolt. With a hand over her mouth and a sudden flurry of arms and legs, she was out of the bed and barging past him on her way to the bathroom.

'Here,' he said quietly, offering her a cool washcloth and a glass of water when, after several dire minutes, she leaned against the tiled wall of the bathroom, feeling totally drained.

'Thanks,' she muttered, beyond embarrassment as she reached gratefully for both offerings.

'Is there anything I can get you? Anything I can do?'

'An undertaker?' she deadpanned, the state of her insides warring with a rising feeling of panic. It was only three weeks and already she was being sick. How on earth was she going to cope with nine months of pregnancy, the inevitable aftermath *and* earn her living?

CHAPTER SIX

'I WANT to see a doctor,' demanded the slurred but still amazingly strident voice that rapidly approached the cubicle where Abby was just finishing tidying up.

'Good morning, Sister. This is Mr Wetherall and he's got a rather unusual problem,' announced the porter, as he wheeled in the vociferous man and winked at Abby out of sight of their rather corpulent patient.

'You're only a nurse,' he accused her on a pungent waft of sour alcoholic fumes, his bleary eyes peering up at her.

Abby's stomach spasmed and nearly revolted at the smell, but she clenched her teeth and her fists and managed to avoid breathing in until the smell had dissipated a bit.

'If you'd like to climb up here,' she suggested, patting the fresh layer of disposable paper sheet she'd just spread over the bed. 'Then we can get you settled before the doctor comes.'

'Can't,' he said, trying to fold his arms and failing to find the necessary co-ordination. 'That's the problem.'

'And what *is* the problem, Mr Wetherall?' she asked politely, using the clipboard that held the start of his case-notes like a shield in front of her. It seemed as if morning sickness had arrived early and with a vengeance, her stomach reacting to a whole series of triggers including coffee, perfume and cigarette smoke. The entire morning had been like negotiating a minefield, and now it seemed that there was alcohol to add to the list of booby-traps.

'You won't be able to do anything to help me,' he declared seriously, his tone full of self-importance as he produced the words one at a time like large wet pebbles. 'Only a nurse. Need a doctor.'

'Tell me anyway,' she said persuasively, 'just so I can write it in our notes.'

She heard the curtain swish open behind her and knew from the strange shiver of awareness along her skin exactly who had come to stand behind her.

'You a doctor?' demanded Mr Wetherall, transferring his attention to a new and obviously more important quarry.

'Yes. I'm Dr Taylor,' Ben said pleasantly. 'Now, what can I do for you?'

'Someone's stolen my kneecaps,' their patient declared with serious outrage, his eyes blinking like those of an owl caught in headlights. 'They've stolen my bleddy kneecaps and I can't stand up. See?'

He made a fumbling attempt at pushing himself upright on the arms of the wheelchair, but his weight was too great and his co-ordination was still almost non-existent.

'I see,' Ben said, apparently in all seriousness, but Abby and the hovering porter could see the fugitive gleam in his eyes as he made the usual meticulous checks to rule out any more serious causes for the problem.

By the time he'd finished it was obvious that the only issue was a serious bout of overindulgence.

'Is cubicle thirteen free, Sister?' Ben asked as he straightened up, referring to the single cubicle at the far end of the department where they could isolate problem patients. 'Perhaps you could organise for him to wait there for tests.'

'See,' Mr Wetherall said, throwing a triumphant glare in Abby's direction as the porter prepared to wheel him along the corridor. 'Doctor knows it's serious. I need tests.'

If he ran true to form Abby knew it wouldn't be long before that end of the department rang with the sound of stertorous snoring as Mr Wetherall slept off the alcohol.

Like many of the others who had occupied that cubicle before him, in a few hours he would wake up with a monumental headache and would be sent on his way, his kneecaps magically restored.

'How are you feeling?' Ben asked quietly, his hazel eyes intent on her.

Abby glanced around, but there was no one near enough to overhear their conversation.

'Better now that he's taken the smell of alcohol away with him,' she murmured with a shudder. 'For a moment there I wasn't certain my breakfast was going to stay with me.'

'I thought you were looking a bit green,' he said with a frown. 'Are you certain you don't need to take some time off?'

'Ben,' she said, forgetting for the moment that they were at work now and that she'd always used the formality of his title before, 'it's a pregnancy, not a terminal illness, and there are more than eight months to go. I've got my living to earn and I can't afford to treat myself like a porcelain doll.'

'Well, forgive me for pointing it out, but at the moment you look about as fragile as a porcelain doll so you'll have to forgive me if I get confused.'

Startled by the unexpected vehemence in his words, Abby stared up at him and saw colour darken his cheek-bones.

'Sorry,' he muttered gruffly, concentrating on tucking his pen inside his pocket as if he couldn't face meeting her eyes.

Suddenly he *did* look at her and his expression was fierce as he leaned towards her, indicating that he'd come to some sort of a decision.

'Abby, we need—*I* need to talk to you. Will you come back to my place again tonight?'

'But we talked for ages last night,' she pointed out, squashing the swift surge of pleasure that flooded through her at his invitation. 'You kept me company until I fell asleep,' she reminded him unnecessarily.

A tingle of nervousness skittered up her spine when she saw how intent he was, and she wondered what else they could possibly have to say to each other.

Her situation wasn't really any of his business as the fingerprints proved he hadn't been involved. Anyway, just because she was attracted to him was no reason why she should take advantage of his good nature.

'That was before,' he began, then seemed to rein in his words hastily.

'Before what?' she demanded, her antennae picking up some very strange vibrations.

'I've been making some enquiries of my own and I've found out some new information. I didn't think you'd want me to tell you about it here while we're on duty.'

For a moment she thought he was using lack of privacy as an excuse to persuade her to stay at his house again, but he looked too serious to be teasing.

'All right,' she agreed nervously. A strange feeling hovered over her that her life was about to undergo another violent change of direction whether she wanted it to or not. 'What time shall I get there?'

'I could give you a lift,' he offered, but her stubborn independent spirit chose that moment to kick in.

'It would be better if I took my car, then you won't have to turn out again to take me home,' she pointed out logically. 'The police confirmed that everything had been made secure after the break-in. I authorised the security company to install new locks all around the flat—doors *and* windows—at the same time.'

'It might be secure, but you aren't seriously intending to stay there, are you? What about the mess?'

His dismay was no greater than her own when she remembered the state of her once-pristine domain.

'I've got to start sorting it out some time and the sooner the better,' she said, hoping her voice sounded more upbeat than she felt. It was a daunting prospect.

The pager clipped to Ben's belt began to bleep, otherwise Abby was sure that he would have continued the argument. She would have been hard-pressed to keep her end up in the dispute if he'd mentioned the fact that at the moment she didn't even have a bed fit to sleep on.

Still, there was the rest of the day to think about that, and it would stop her having time to think about the other problem in her life. At least, it *would* stop her thinking about it if only she didn't feel so sick all the time.

A beckoning hand told her that she probably wasn't going to have time to think about anything except her job, and she hurried towards the other end of the row of curtained cubicles.

Her arrival coincided with that of a distraught young woman in a wheelchair, her arms wrapped convulsively around herself as she sobbed.

'Sister Walker, this is Lucille Pike and she's—' The ambulanceman never had a chance to finish his introduction.

'I'm losing my baby,' she sobbed. 'Don't let me lose my baby.'

It felt as if a tight fist clutched at Abby's heart in sympathy with the woman's distress, and suddenly she knew without question that there was no way she could get rid of her own baby.

It might owe its conception to an act of violence, but the act of getting rid of the tangible evidence wouldn't take away the memory of it. In fact, with her upbringing and beliefs, it might actually make it worse.

While her thoughts were whirling in her head her hands were working automatically to assist the young woman out of the wheelchair and onto the bed.

'How many weeks pregnant are you?' Abby asked, as she slipped Mrs Pike's shoes off and helped her off with her jacket.

'I should be about three and a half months but I had a sort of a period a couple of times at about the time my period would have been. I read in a book that it sometimes happens.' She looked at Abby for confirmation but she was more interested in getting the facts.

'Has your doctor confirmed the pregnancy yet or have you just done one of those home tester kits?'

'I didn't need to do either,' she said with a tearful smile. 'We'd been trying for over six months without any success, but then my periods virtually disappeared like that and I just knew. When I started to show—

you know, my tummy started getting bigger—well, I'm working full time and I didn't want to lose any money by taking time off for doctor's visits. We're going to need every penny if we're going to be able to give the baby what he needs. That's why my husband is working away on the oil rigs.'

'What have you got for me?' murmured a deep voice in Abby's ear. She smiled and handed her notes over to Ben without a tremor. It seemed as if, having made her decision about her own baby, she'd been suffused with new strength and determination.

By this time Abby had quietly settled a blanket over her patient and had written the essential details on the form.

'Unconfirmed pregnancy of unconfirmed duration. Now suffering pain and loss of blood.' She kept her voice calm as she relayed the basic information, but couldn't help her instinctive feeling of sympathy for the woman's distress.

She stood by quietly as Ben conducted his examination and drew up a blood sample while they waited for the ultrasound equipment to arrive.

'It's the quickest way of finding out what's happening in there,' Ben explained gently. 'If there's a baby there and the heart's beating we'll actually be able to see it on the screen.'

Abby realised that his explanation had been slanted towards what the young woman expected to hear, but she knew from the frown pleating his forehead that he was also considering other possibilities.

Apart from any of the variations of ectopic pregnancy, her symptoms could also be indicative of fibroids, cysts or even certain forms of cancer. The only way he would be able to narrow the field was by taking a look.

'Can I see?' she begged, grasping at Abby's arm when the technician arrived to set everything up.

'We need to let her get everything running to make sure she gets a clear picture,' Abby explained, as she helped the young woman slip her clothing out of the way and applied a dollop of gel to the soft swell of her belly.

Ben was standing behind the technician, his eyes fixed firmly on the screen as she began to stroke the probe backwards and forwards to establish the field of the examination.

Abby's eyes were fixed firmly on him and she knew that all was not well. Her heart sank. There had been very little change in his expression, certainly not enough for their patient to see, but she'd spent several months watching him now.

His murmured direction was spoken too softly for either Abby or Lucille Pike to hear, but when Abby saw the way the probe was directed to the region where the ovary and Fallopian tube would be she realised that the list of options was narrowing.

'Well? Is my baby all right?' demanded the young woman, half in eagerness and half in dread. 'Can I see?'

'Mrs Pike, I'm afraid there isn't a baby to show you,' Ben began gently.

'No baby?' she gasped. 'But...how? I haven't bled enough to have lost him already. Are you sure?'

'I'm sure.' His hazel eyes were full of sympathy as he perched on the edge of the bed beside her. 'It looks as if you haven't actually been pregnant at all,' he continued, directing her gaze towards the screen the technician had angled in her direction.

'Not pregnant?' she said disbelievingly. 'But what about my periods? And...and the baby's been growing...'

'What it looks like is an ovarian cyst,' Ben explained gently, one long finger outlining the extent of the problem. 'That could explain all the problems you've been having—the difficulty conceiving, the spotty bleeding, the growth.'

'How can you get rid of it? Will this mean you have to operate to take everything away? A...a hysterectomy? Does this mean I won't be able to have any children? Is it cancer?' The questions poured out one after the other, without allowing any time for answers, her fears more evident with each one.

'Yes, it will mean an operation,' Ben confirmed when she finally ran out of breath and lay looking up at him, with tears sliding silently into her hair as they poured out of her eyes.

'Until the surgeon has a look in there we can't tell you for certain whether there's any cancer involved, but I don't think it's very likely. The surgeon will take samples during the operation and send them up to the lab to make certain. Even then he won't know until he actually looks at it whether he can save the ovary or if leaving it in there will just be an invitation to more trouble later on.'

'But—'

'As for the rest,' he hurried on when she began to interrupt, 'once you've had your all-clear you'd certainly be able to go on and try for a family with only one working ovary—plenty of women do. It just means that the eggs will be ripened and released on the same side every month.'

'So I'll still be able to have a family?' she asked, her eyes begging for reassurance.

'If everything else in there is in full working order, then removing one ovary shouldn't stop you getting pregnant. As I said, once your doctor gives you the all-clear after you've recovered from the operation, he'll be able to give you the most up-to-date advice about the best and quickest way of achieving it.'

'Is there special advice?' she asked hesitantly, her expression halfway between curiosity and embarrassment.

'Oh, yes,' Ben confirmed. 'Two unbreakable rules that you and your husband will have to follow. Firstly, you have to make love and, secondly, you have to do it often.'

There was a brief surprised silence before the young woman chuckled. 'Oh, I think my husband will be willing to help me with that,' she confirmed with a watery smile, 'but first I've got to tell him that he can stop pretending to have sympathetic cravings for chocolate and ice cream at three o'clock in the morning.'

Ben patted her hand as he joined in the laughter. Abby couldn't help feeling a glow of pride when she saw the way he'd managed to turn Lucille's mind from her present fear and disappointment to a more hopeful, and enjoyable future.

She knew, without a shadow of doubt, that he would applaud her own decision not to have an abortion, and knew, too, that over the coming months he would keep an eye on her to make sure that she was safe and well.

There was one big disappointment that she hadn't yet let herself contemplate. The fledgling attraction that had sparked between the two of them when they'd first met might once have had a chance to grow into something wonderful and permanent. *That* now seemed to have withered away under the onslaught of circumstances.

'Asleep on your feet, Sister?' teased Ben, and made her jump. Suddenly she realised that she was standing there with an armful of crumpled paper sheet. Heaven only knew how long she'd been staring into the distance while her mind went walkabout.

'Uh, no. I was just…thinking,' she mumbled, as she hurriedly stuffed it in the bin and turned to pull a fresh length of sheet over the bed.

'Well, we've got a special treat this time,' he said with more than a hint of laughter in his voice. 'He can't move very fast but he should be arriving any minute.'

Abby frowned and stuck her head out to look along the corridor. Making his painful way towards her was a strapping young man in his late teens or early twenties.

Her frown deepened as she watched the way he was walking. It was vaguely reminiscent of the way a toddler coped with nappy rash.

When he saw Abby he stopped dead.

'She's not going to be here, is she?' he demanded, his face suffused with a furious blush.

'Not only that but she's going to be doing most of the work,' Ben confirmed, and Abby wondered exactly what was going on when she saw the wicked glint in his eye.

'If you'd like to get your things off and lie down on the bed…on your stomach,' Ben directed, as he pulled the curtain across and enclosed the three of them in the close confines of the cubicle.

'But...you're not going to watch!' he exclaimed, clearly horrified.

'We're going to have to do more than watch,' Ben pointed out. 'You've already told me that you had a go on your own and couldn't manage.'

Abby was intrigued but took pity on him and turned her back, pretending to find something urgent to do while the sound of rustling clothing went on behind her.

There were several sharp hisses of pain, and from Ben's mutter she gathered that he was lending some practical assistance.

'Right, Sister. How good are you with tweezers?'

'Pretty accurate,' she said as she turned back, then she stared. 'Ouch! What happened to you?'

'I...er...had an accident,' the young man mumbled into his folded arms, the back of his neck and his ears scarlet with embarrassment.

'But this looks like—'

'Duck or grouse?' suggested Ben with a wicked chuckle. 'And the season doesn't start until the twelfth of August.'

There was a groan from the top of the bed.

'If this is a gunshot wound, we have to inform the police, don't we?' she asked as she poured antiseptic solution into a bowl and brought it across to the bed.

'Already done it,' said their patient through his teeth as Abby began to irrigate the array of very angry-looking puncture wounds that marked the scatter of shotgun pellets. 'There was a copper in Reception and I gave him all the details. He's got to fill in a mountain of forms about it.'

'So, what did happen?' Abby prompted, as she settled herself down to probe as gently as she could for the ball-bearing-sized pieces of metal embedded in the flesh of his buttocks and thighs.

'I...er...dropped my gun and it went off accidentally,' he said, the words sounding suspiciously well rehearsed.

Abby had a feeling that was the story he'd concocted for the police. She wouldn't be at all surprised if the truth was very different.

'What do you do that involves handling guns?' she asked, and smiled, wondering if he realised how obvious it was from her viewpoint that the way she hadn't pursued the explanation had made him relax.

'Farming,' he said succinctly. 'Dad and me work the farm together but I also do extra for neighbours when they need a hand.'

It was a time-consuming job, punctuated by the satisfaction of dropping each pellet with a resounding clatter into the metal dish. Unfortunately, several of them were deeply enough embedded that she'd needed to numb the area with an injection of anaesthetic before she could extract the offending objects.

The whole thing was made worse by the fact that they'd now been there for over a day while he'd tried unsuccessfully to extract them himself, and several sites were looking very angry.

By the time she'd finished, young Jason had loosened up enough to spill the beans about his ongoing relationship with Sarah, the pretty daughter of one of their neighbours.

'Her father doesn't think I'm good enough for her because I do labouring for him,' he said tightly, as he rolled over and gingerly sat up. 'Wouldn't listen when she tried to tell him that I've been to agricultural college and I own half of our farm.'

Abby now had a good idea how Jason had *really* received his injuries.

'Came after you, did he?' she hazarded, and the expression on his face told her she'd scored her own bull's-eye. She laughed. 'Played right into your hands, didn't he?' she said.

He frowned. 'How?'

'You mean that isn't why you told that story to the police?'

'I told them that so Sarah wouldn't be involved. I love her and want to marry her. I don't want her to get a bad name.'

'So you haven't figured out yet that you can actually use the situation to get what you want?' Abby prompted slyly.

'How? He caught me sneaking away from the farm after she'd been with me in the barn. Said he'd do me for trespassing.'

'If you were to inform the police that he'd shot you, he'd be in a lot of trouble…'

'Well, that certainly wouldn't gain me a lot of points,' he objected.

'No, but if you only threatened to? By the sound of him, he's the sort who'll care what other people think of him and with your Sarah on your side you can probably use the threat as leverage to get him to agree to your marriage.'

He was thoughtful for a moment then his face cleared and was taken over by a delighted grin.

'Do you know, that almost makes it worthwhile going through this.' He gestured towards his sore posterior. 'I can't wait to get home and put things in motion.'

'Not so fast.' Abby grabbed his elbow. 'First you've got an appointment up in X-Ray to make sure I got it all out, and then you've got a prescription to pick up for antibiotics. And while we're on a roll, when was the last time you updated your tetanus cover?'

'Ah, you're not going to get the chance to stick me with one of those. My last one was only six months ago—one of *his* cows head-butted me and I had to have stitches.' He lifted his thick thatch of hair and pointed to a neat scar on his forehead. 'Bled like crazy. Looked like something out of a horror film, but my Sarah didn't bat an eyelid,' he said with a mixture of pride and relish.

'Gruesome beast,' Abby complained, and flapped a hand at him to send him on his way. 'Oh, and, Jason, good luck,' she added, and was rewarded by another of his infectious grins.

'I'll send you a piece of cake,' he promised, and hobbled off, following the signs towards the X-ray department.

'He seems a lot happier,' Ben commented as he joined her in the corridor. 'Any problems?'

'He's just off for an X-ray, but otherwise everything's OK.' She glanced down at her watch. 'Time for my break,' she announced, and had to quell a sudden lurch of pleasure when he matched his stride to hers and set off in the same direction.

It seemed strange not to be making herself a coffee, and she actually had to hold her breath when Ben poured boiling water over instant granules and the pungent aroma drifted her way.

Would she ever be able to smell coffee again without feeling sick?

'So, what was that young Jason said about cake?' he demanded as he hooked his foot round an empty chair and dragged it across to join the one she'd seized. 'I thought the saying was something about an apple a day. Did you have to bribe him to hold still?'

Abby laughed. 'No bribery, but I think I might just have involved myself in another illegal activity,' she said ruefully.

'You mean he admitted there was more to the wound than the accident he reported to the police?' Ben said with a frown. 'Was he attacked? Do you need to have a word with them about it?'

'Yes and no,' she said with a chuckle. 'Yes, there was more to it and, no, I don't think I need to speak to the police. What I meant was that I was aiding and abetting him in the planning of a blackmail attempt on the man he hopes is going to be his future father-in-law.'

'His…?' Words failed him. 'You don't mean *he* was the one who shot Jason?'

'In an attempt at *avoiding* becoming his father-in-law,' Abby explained. 'But it looks as if he's just handed the two of them the weapon to guarantee his agreement.'

'And I bet Jason hadn't realised it until your devious mind latched onto it and pointed it out to him,' Ben said, and Abby couldn't help her triumphant grin.

'I have had a little practice,' she admitted, as memories surfaced of her attempts at smoothing her brother's romantic path.

'My father was against my brother getting married. He was twenty-eight and still Dad said he was too young and kept putting up all sorts of objections to delay it. Basically, he thought Trish wasn't nearly high-powered enough for his high-flying son, but she was exactly what my brother needed—someone with her feet firmly on the ground who can keep everything calm around him while his mega-brain solves global puzzles.'

'What did you do—or daren't I ask?' The warm hazel eyes were fixed on her face but she could feel treacherous heat spreading right through her body. It took a real effort to recall his question and give an answer.

'I suggested they told him that Trish was pregnant with their first grandchild and see if he tried to get rid of her then,' Abby said simply.

'And what happened?'

'Mum couldn't push them up the aisle fast enough! She only stopped knitting little white things long enough to get through the reception.'

'And?' he prompted, and she realised that he seemed to be able to see through her attempt at a poker face as easily as she could read him. The thought that their minds seemed to be working on similar lines caused her a pang if she let herself think about what might have been.

Still, if all they could have was a close working relationship, that was better than nothing.

'And the baby arrived eighteen months later,' she finished with a grin.

'Eighteen...?'

'Well, I only suggested that they *told* Dad she was pregnant, not that they actually rushed into making it a fact. That would be the last reason for starting a pregnancy or a marriage.'

'As I said. A devious woman,' he commented, raising his cup towards her. 'And are they happy?'

'Blissfully. My brother's too wrapped up in his work and my sister-in-law's too level-headed to let my parents get too far under their skin. They seem to have worked out the perfect balance.'

Silence fell between them, but it was a comfortable one that allowed Abby to relax and savour Ben's company.

A colleague called across, and while Ben replied Abby took advantage of the fact that his attention was drawn away to feast her eyes on him.

The more she looked at him and the more she got to know him, the more she wondered how she could possibly have mistaken anyone else for him.

Perhaps it had been the aura of secrecy with which his double had surrounded their meetings that had blinded her to the many differences between them—differences that now seemed blatantly obvious.

There were long hours left of the day before she was due to meet him at his house, and by the time she reached the end of her shift her stomach was in turmoil—not from morning sickness this time, although the threat of that never seemed to be far away.

For all Ben's light-hearted repartee that day she had seen a core of serious intent in his eyes when he'd looked at her and she wondered exactly what he wanted to talk about.

'Not much longer and you'll know,' she muttered, as she fished for the keys in the bottom of her bag, glad of the long, light evenings at this time of the year. Life was so much nicer when you didn't have to arrive at work in darkness and leave again to find the same darkness waiting for you.

She was standing right beside her car before she noticed anything was wrong, and even then she couldn't believe what she was seeing.

All along the side of the vehicle someone had taken a sharp object—maybe a knife or even a key—and had scratched the same obscenities as had been painted on her bedroom walls.

And as if that wasn't bad enough, as she gazed in horror at the extent of the damage she realised that both tyres were flat, the jagged gashes in their sides mute testimony as to what had happened.

Suddenly she had a feeling that someone was looking at her and all the hairs went up on the back of her neck.

When she heard the sound of approaching footsteps her heart began to pound with fear as the memory of her attacker's fury rose up in her mind's eye and she froze, too scared to move.

There was just time for her to wish that she'd accepted Ben's offer of a lift before a hand grasped her shoulder and whirled her to face him.

CHAPTER SEVEN

'ABBY. Are you all right?'

'Ben,' she breathed shakily, her legs no stronger than over-cooked spaghetti as she went from terror to relief in a split second.

Then anger roared through her.

'Don't you *ever* do that again,' she shrieked, suddenly out of control as she flung his hand away from her and whirled to face him. 'Creeping up on me... grabbing me...scaring me out of my wits...'

As quickly as it had come the anger was gone, and with it any pretence at strength or self-control as she burst into tears and threw herself against him.

'Oh, Ben, I'm sorry,' she wailed, immeasurably relieved when she felt his arms around her to hold her securely against him. One hand cradled her head against his shoulder while the other stroked her back in a slow, soothing rhythm.

An image flashed into her head of the young baby he'd held earlier that day while her mother's hand had been cleaned up and prepared for stitching.

The little one had obviously known that all was not right with her world and had grizzled solidly in her mother's free arm while Ben had examined the wound to make certain that no major tendons, veins or nerves had been damaged.

Once it had just been a matter of letting Abby get on with the job, he'd scooped the child up from her mother's lap and had begun to walk backwards and forwards in the limited space of the cubicle.

Within moments his deep voice, murmuring nonsense, seemed to have mesmerised the little girl into silence, while the soft, stroking motion up and down her back had soon comforted her enough to send her to sleep.

Abby could empathise with the feeling. If she stayed in his arms much longer she'd be falling asleep too.

'I'm sorry,' she repeated, as she fumbled in her pocket for a tissue.

'Nothing to apologise for,' he said, as he offered his own handkerchief. 'I should have said something so you'd know who I was.'

'Even so,' she argued, then had to stop when he placed one fingertip on her lips.

'Forget it,' he advised softly. 'We've more important things to sort out.' His hazel gaze left her and travelled over her shoulder to her car.

'I take it you recognise the signature,' he commented dryly, and she saw him inspecting the state of the paintwork and tyres. 'Do you want to go back into the hospital to phone the police or shall we do it from my place?'

The thought of having to go back into A and E and hang around until the police could take a statement, or whatever they needed to do, was daunting. All she really wanted to do was get away from here—far enough away that she'd be able to forget about it, even if only for a few hours.

'Take me home,' Abby whispered, and only realised what she'd said when his eyebrows drew together into a sharp frown and he drew back so that she was at arm's length.

'Home? But we were supposed to be having that talk.'

Suddenly she realised that her own flat didn't feel like home any more in spite of all the time and effort she'd put into it. She'd only spent a few hours in Ben's house, but in spite of the improvements still to be done she'd felt as if she belonged there.

'Actually, I meant your home,' she murmured, hoping he wouldn't notice the start of a blush heating her cheeks.

'Good,' he said, cheerful once more as he turned and guided her towards his car. 'You don't mind if we do a quick detour to shop? I haven't had time to do any for several days and I think the cupboard's bare apart from some milk and the last crust of the bread.'

They were both laughing by the time Ben struggled to put the key in his front door, both of them with their arms laden with shopping.

'I defy *anyone* to do anything worthwhile with low-fat cream cheese,' he challenged. 'The only thing that has *less* flavour is limp lettuce.'

'You wait and see,' Beth retorted, as her hunger returned for the first time in what felt like weeks. 'You'll eat your words as well as the cream cheese.'

Ben was still muttering uncomplimentary things about her choice of menu as he left her in the kitchen. She'd shooed him out and told him to make himself useful by carrying the rest of the bags to his spare room then making the damage report to the police.

When her hands were busy with mixing the despised cream cheese with salt, pepper, lemon juice and a hint of garlic, and stuffing it into the pockets she'd created in plump, skinless chicken breasts, she finally admitted to herself that she really had no option but to accept Ben's offer of hospitality.

A shiver travelled up her spine when she thought about the evidence of violence still scattered throughout her flat and added it to the damage done to her car.

She really wasn't safe until whoever was stalking her was caught—and there was nowhere that she felt safer than here, with Ben.

The meal was a rousing success, and when Ben cleaned his plate with obvious relish she took great delight in saying, 'I told you so.'

She had almost managed to forget the problems surrounding her during the fun of clean-up duty, but when Ben suggested they went through to the sitting room to talk, the newly serious expression on his face robbed her of her temporary gaiety.

She settled herself on one end of the settee and tried to bolster herself with a silent pep talk while she waited for him to join her.

A moment later he was there, and her heart beat out a nervous tattoo as he leaned forward to present her with a steaming mug of coffee.

In an instant she was out of her seat and racing for the bathroom, sweat popping out all over her skin when it seemed as if she would never get there in time.

'Oh-h-h, yuck!' she groaned endless miserable minutes later as she leaned weakly against the cool tiles, trembling from head to foot.

'Here,' said a concerned voice behind her, and a glass of water appeared over her shoulder.

A small part of her cringed at the thought that Ben was seeing her like this, her face still green and clammy after depositing her meal in his toilet. Mostly, though, she was just grateful that he was there to take care of her. She didn't feel as if she could summon up the energy to do it for herself.

She rinsed her mouth with water that had never tasted sweeter, then accepted the washcloth he offered to wipe her face and hands.

'Finished?' he prompted.

'God, I hope so,' she said with feeling. 'Any more and I'll be bringing up the soles of my feet.'

She heard a snort of suppressed laughter behind her but couldn't be bothered to tell him off for being unsympathetic when he was helping her to her feet and wrapping an arm around her shoulders for support.

'Do you want me to carry you?' he offered, and she took back the mental accusation of lack of sympathy.

'I can walk,' she asserted, squashing down the mental image of Rhett Butler sweeping a beautiful Scarlett O'Hara off her feet and substituting her own, far less impressive green-round-the-gills self.

Perhaps it would be different if he was offering to carry her to the bedroom for a night of bliss, but all she felt capable of at the moment was collapsing in a heap and sleeping.

'Oh, Ben, I can't turn you out of your bed again,' she objected when she saw he'd guided her into his own room and she caught sight of the bags containing the start of her new wardrobe scattered across his bed. 'Let me sleep in your spare room.'

'I would if I had one,' he said with a rather sheepish expression on his face.

'What?' Abby wasn't certain what she was hearing. 'But where were you sleeping last night before I woke you up with my nightmare?'

'Who said I was sleeping?' he asked dryly, and she felt even more guilty.

'That's crazy,' she objected, and turned to stalk out. 'I can curl up on your settee for the night. You need to sleep properly if you're going to be able to work tomorrow.'

'I worked far longer hours without sleep during my training,' he pointed out, as he caught up with her and dragged her gently but inexorably back into the room. 'Anyway, how much sleep do you think I'd get if I knew you were down there?'

'So we've reached stalemate, have we?' she demanded, tilting her chin at a combative angle.

'Stalemate or a point of compromise.'

'What compromise?' Her heart started to tap out a staccato rhythm when she realised how few compromises there were at this time of night. She wouldn't even allow herself to admit the first one that sprang to mind, especially when she realised how intently Ben was watching her.

'Well,' he began, his voice taking on a husky tone, 'it seems to me that we managed to share last time without you stealing all the covers. We could try it again.'

Nervous excitement froze the words of agreement in her throat long enough for her to have second thoughts. It was obviously long enough for Ben to take it as a signal of refusal.

'You wouldn't have to worry that I'd...er...try anything,' he added quickly, and the worried expression in his eyes, combined with the sight of the deepening colour over his cheek-bones, was enough to loosen her tongue.

'I trust you, Ben,' she whispered, needing to rid him

of any hint to the contrary, 'but whether I trust you not to steal the covers is another matter.'

Her teasing comment was enough to break the tension between them, but as they took turns to prepare to go to sleep tension of a completely different sort seemed to crackle in the air.

Abby took advantage of Ben's trip downstairs to check the locks to slide quickly under the covers.

Her new T-shirt-style nightwear was perfectly decent—not nearly as transparent as Ben's much-washed offering last night—but the way her breasts were pointedly announcing her awareness that she was soon going to be sharing his bed was not something she was ready to reveal.

She expected him to come straight up again, but as the house settled into silence she heard the opening chords of the same piece of guitar music drifting up the stairs.

The realisation that Ben was allowing her time alone to go to sleep demolished the wall of anxiety she'd begun to build up around herself, and with the tension gone she was able to allow the rippling notes to soothe her until she felt herself drifting peacefully into sleep.

'Abby,' a sleep-roughened voice murmured in her ear, and she groaned her displeasure at the interruption, not wanting to surface from the warm, fuzzy depths of her dream.

She was imagining that she was in bed with Ben Taylor, her head cradled on his naked chest and his arms wrapped around her to hold their bodies as close as if they were two halves of a whole.

She'd been having variations of this dream ever

since the wretched man had come to work at St Augustine's, but this was certainly the most vivid yet. Why, she could almost feel the heat radiating from his body and hear his heartbeat thumping out an urgent rhythm under her ear.

As for the hair scattered across his chest, she could almost swear that she could feel the way it tickled the palm of her hand as she traced the broad inverted triangle down over the flat muscled belly towards—

'Abby!' Now there was a warning tone to the voice as a lean masculine hand captured her own and halted its tantalising progress.

Abby froze, suddenly realising with a flood of mortification that she wasn't still wrapped in a dream. Ben *was* in the bed with her and the hand he'd trapped under his own had trespassed just inches from—

'Oh, God,' she groaned, and turned to bury her head in her pillow—except it wasn't her pillow but the warm muscular planes of Ben's broad chest that she encountered.

Embarrassed beyond belief, she scooted backwards out of his arms and rolled away across the bed.

Unfortunately, the sudden movement didn't sit well with her stomach and the next moment she was up and running for the bathroom.

By the time her misery had subsided and she'd emerged from the bathroom Ben had disappeared downstairs. Abby grabbed a selection of her new clothes and dragged them quickly over her trembling body.

'Toast,' Ben announced, offering her a plate bearing a couple of perfectly cooked slices as she appeared in the doorway. 'I'll leave you to decide if you want to put anything on them. The kettle's just boiled for you to make yourself a drink or there's a selection of alternatives in the fridge.'

He paused in the doorway for a moment, his eyes going swiftly over her in what seemed to be a totally professional assessment before he gave a single nod and disappeared on his way up the stairs.

Abby breathed a sigh of relief and began to nibble tentatively. As soon as she realised that the nausea had gone for the moment she ate hungrily. It seemed like days since she'd had a meal—at least a meal that had stayed with her—and her body was craving nourishment for the tiny life developing inside.

'Feeling better?' Ben asked when he reappeared. He was dressed for work in a pair of dark trousers and a pale blue shirt, his suit jacket hooked over one finger. His dark hair was even darker with the residual dampness of his shower and still bore the furrows that marked his use of a comb to tame a tendency to curls.

'Much,' she agreed gratefully, and sighed as she sat back in her chair.

'Enough to listen while I give you the news I should have told you last night?' He deposited his jacket on top of the fridge and turned his chair around to straddle it, his arms folded across the back to stretch his cotton shirt tightly over the width of his shoulders.

Abby dragged her gaze back to his face and the serious expression in his eyes killed the unaccustomed excitement that had started to build inside her.

She licked her lips as tension of a different sort gripped her. 'What is it? What's happened?' she whispered.

'Nothing major,' he said, obviously trying to reassure her, 'but there are several... Oh, hell,' he explained, raking his fingers through his hair in exasperation and messing up his meticulous grooming, 'I never have been any good at beating about the bush. The DNA results have come back.'

'And?' Abby swallowed as her breakfast settled uneasily in a stomach suddenly filled with unease.

'And they're identical,' he said baldly.

'Identical?' Abby parroted softly. The implications were too momentous to grasp for a moment and she found herself focusing on the way the skin over Ben's knuckles had turned white when he'd tightened them into fists. 'You mean somewhere, not very far away, you've got an identical twin you've never known about?'

He didn't reply, and she had the feeling that he was waiting for her to say something more.

'Oh, Ben, how did it happen? How did you become separated? How could your mother not *know* that she'd had twins?'

Ben closed his eyes and gave a silent chuckle. It had been hours ago since he'd broken the news about the DNA results to Abby and he still couldn't help marvelling at her response.

He'd been so worried that her faith in his innocence would be dented by the results, but she hadn't hesitated for a moment, making the leap from acceptance to questioning *how* it could have happened almost in the same breath.

He drained his coffee and slumped back into his chair, glad of a few moments to gather his thoughts and his strength.

This morning had been dreadful. The first patient through the door as he'd started his shift had been an overweight, middle-aged man who'd collapsed when he'd tried to run for a train. The state of his cardiovascular system made it very unlikely that he'd survive in spite of his relative youth and their best efforts.

They'd hardly drawn breath after that one when a teenager had been rushed in by his mother in a diabetic coma, followed immediately by an elderly gentleman with electrical burns.

The teenager was easy to deal with. He was unfortunately becoming a regular visitor as he went through a teenage rebellion against his condition and tried to do without his insulin injections.

He was going to have to stay on the ward until he'd been properly stabilised again. Hopefully, this time his rather close brush with death would persuade him that life as a diabetic was better than no life at all.

The elderly gentleman was another problem altogether. Recently widowed, he'd put an old electric blanket on the bed to counteract the empty chill of his missing partner, not realising that the wiring was dangerous.

He'd fallen asleep with the blanket still switched on and 'had an accident' in the night. The mixture of urine and bare electrical wires meant he'd ended up with severe burns right around one hip.

Ben's mouth tightened when he remembered the elderly man's confusion and embarrassment. Not only was he in severe pain and with the prospect of a long hospital stay while essential skin grafts were done, he was mortified that a pretty young nurse was having to perform such essential intimacies as washing him.

He smiled as he remembered the way Abby had put his mind at rest.

'Now, Arthur,' she'd said. 'I'm going to wash up

as far as possible and down as far as possible, then I'll give you the cloth and you can wash possible.'

It had taken a moment before Arthur had grasped her meaning but the smile of relief that had washed over his face had made Ben very proud of her sensitivity to an old man's pride.

He should have known she'd be like that. Just this morning she'd sat quietly and listened while he'd revealed the story of his early childhood.

Most of the information had been new to him, only revealed by his adoptive parents when he'd told them about the DNA results.

The fact that his mother's health history had precluded her from bearing children of her own had also prejudiced the usual adoption agencies. As a result his adoption had been a private one, and the fact that his natural mother had completely disappeared after handing over her child had never struck them as suspicious before.

Now Philip and Helen Taylor were doing everything they could to unravel the mystery, his mother in particular mourning the fact that she'd missed the chance to rear the twins together. Had she done so, could it be that nurture would have outweighed nature and turned his other half into a completely different person?

The door swung open and snapped Ben out of his introspection. There was nothing he could do at the moment, other than hope that Abby would put her fierce independence aside long enough to allow him to keep her safe.

If he had his way he'd like to do far more than just keep her safe, but the prospect of deepening their relationship was going to have to wait for a more propitious time.

'Oh. Hello, Ben.'

Abby heard the strain in her voice and silently cursed the fact that, of all people, she had to meet up with Ben now—before she'd had a chance to recover from her shock.

'Abby? What's the matter?'

He was up out of his seat in a flash and by her side almost before she could draw breath.

'Sit down before you fall down.' He guided her into a chair and crouched beside her to look up into her face. 'Tell me what happened,' he demanded insistently, as he captured both trembling hands in his.

Abby shut her eyes and drew in a deep breath as she drew new strength from the simple contact between them.

'I had a phone call,' she said, when she thought she had her voice under control. 'He phoned me here, at St Augustine's. The man who—'

Ben's mouth tightened into a thin line.

'Well, we always knew that he realised where you worked,' he said patiently. 'And it would be relatively easy to get a call switched through to A and E. I suppose he got fed up with leaving messages at your flat.'

'He said...he said I had to go home some time,' she said, trying to forget the foul words he'd called her for sleeping away from home and the implications he'd drawn. As if she *could* have slept in her flat after he'd destroyed everything in it. And as if Ben could be interested in her that way.

Not only had she accused him of rape but now, purely out of the goodness of his heart, he'd become involved in all the less than attractive aftermath. He'd be glad when she got herself on her feet again and stopped leaning on him. So would she, she reminded herself sternly, refusing to think about the wonderful feeling of security that surrounded her when he offered his support.

'It wouldn't have been so bad if I hadn't just had another bout of morning sickness. I'm sure I'd have been able to cope with it if he hadn't caught me at a bad time.'

'Abby.' There was new determination in Ben's voice as he said her name and his gaze was very intent as it met hers head on, his hands tightening around hers.

'When are you going to admit that you're in a very vulnerable position at the moment, especially when you live alone? There isn't ever going to be a *good* time for that sort of phone call, never mind the threats he's making. What happens if the police can't find him? How long is he going to keep terrorising you? What happens if it's still going on when the baby arrives?'

'Don't, Ben,' she pleaded. 'You're just making it worse. At some point I've still got to go home and pick up the threads of my life—or rather the threads of my new life.'

'That's not strictly true,' he pointed out. 'There's no reason why you *should* have to go home and face it all alone.'

'Oh, Ben,' Abby sighed when she realised what he was offering. She wished there was some way she could take him up on his suggestion. 'I can't become a permanent lodger in your house. It wouldn't be fair to you.'

Ben smiled wryly and there was a flash of emotion

in his eyes which was swiftly hidden under the sweep of his dark lashes. Then he looked up again, once more in perfect control.

'Actually, I wasn't suggesting a tenancy,' he said, then threw an exasperated glance towards the door as voices approached. 'What I was suggesting was that you should marry me.'

CHAPTER EIGHT

ABBY gaped at Ben as he knelt beside her, unable to believe what she'd heard him say.

Before she could ask, a group of colleagues entered the room and called a greeting. Ben hastily regained his feet so there was no time to ask—no time to talk at all.

He was waiting for her at the end of her shift and she knew there was no point in objecting when he turned his car automatically towards his house. Why object when the only thing she'd been able to think about was finding out what he'd meant? Anyway, until she sorted out the mess at her house she didn't really have anywhere else to go.

'What did you mean?' she demanded baldly, whirling to face him when the front door closed behind them. She was too wound up to spare the time for social niceties.

'I would have thought it was fairly obvious,' he returned mildly, walking around her and disappearing into the kitchen.

'But…but you said marriage!' she exclaimed as she followed in his wake, frustrated that he didn't seem to be treating the situation in the least bit seriously.

'You must admit, the idea does have certain advantages in your situation,' he said, his back towards her as he filled the kettle and set it to heat.

'My situation?' Her words held a demand for clarification.

Ben finally turned to face her, leaning back against the work surface and crossing his feet at the ankles as calmly as if they were discussing nothing more earth-shattering than the weather.

'You're pregnant,' he started, ticking off one long finger. 'You're virtually homeless.' A second finger joined it. 'You're being stalked—probably by my twin brother, who is also probably the person who raped you.' He raised a third finger to join the other two. 'You're short of sleep because of the nightmares and short on nutrition because of the sickness.' He held up his outstretched hand, all five digits raised. 'In short, you need someone to take care of you.'

Her hackles came up at the suggestion that she wasn't capable of taking care of herself. She'd been on her own ever since her parents had moved to New Zealand, and until the last month she'd coped perfectly well.

He must have anticipated her outrage because he continued quickly. 'Last, but definitely not least, we seem to like each other and get on well together. I think we'd be good for each other.'

Startled beyond belief at his unexpected assertion, the strength disappeared from her knees. Abby subsided onto a chair and stared at him.

The naked sincerity in his voice and in his hazel eyes had completely taken the wind out of her sails, and all she could think about was the warmth that seeped through her every time he quietly insisted on taking care of her. And he did, genuinely, seem to care.

Why was another matter altogether.

Was it pity? She'd certainly seen plenty of evidence of his compassion since they'd started working together. Was it misplaced guilt because he was genetically linked to the cause of all her problems?

She was silent for a long time while she looked at him, trying to read from his expression what had prompted him to suggest such an outlandish solution, but for once he was like a closed book.

A small, tight knot of panic started to grow inside her chest as she contemplated the outcome of her two possible answers.

If she turned him down, would that be the end of the friendship between them? She had so enjoyed the relaxed atmosphere between them in the time they'd spent together, in spite of the fact that a large proportion of it recently seemed to have been spent with her head hanging over a toilet.

But was it fair to him to accept? None of this was his fault so why should he feel that it was his place to pay the penalty?

On the other hand, there was that spark that had kindled between them when they'd first met and, whatever had happened in between, it was still there. On her side, at least, she had a feeling that it wouldn't take much for the spark to ignite into an inferno.

'Please, Abby,' Ben said. His soft words drew her out of her introspection in time to see him crouch beside her again, his hands capturing hers in a warm grasp that sent a strange tingle all the way to her depths. 'Give me a chance. Let me show you that you can trust me to take care of you—and the baby.'

It was quite frightening how quickly everything happened once Ben put his mind to it.

It was only three days since she'd whispered her hesitant agreement—well, what else could she do when she'd seen in his eyes just how much he'd wanted her to? How could she do anything other than tell him that he was the most trustworthy man she'd ever known?

Now there were butterflies practising dive-bombing raids in her stomach and they weren't helping the nausea, which hadn't subsided in spite of the fact that she hadn't managed to hang on to her breakfast.

'Are you ready, dear?' prompted a voice at Abby's elbow, and when she turned to meet the clear blue-grey gaze of Celia MacDonald she had a feeling that it wasn't the first time she'd spoken.

Abby gulped and nodded, her clammy hands tightening around her small bouquet of fragrant freesias as she turned to face the silent man standing at her other side in the strangely sterile waiting room.

'Shall we?' He held out his arm and waited for her to place her hand on it.

Abby saw the tremor in her chilly fingers, and when he covered them with his own much warmer ones she knew he'd seen it, too.

'It's not too late to change your mind,' he murmured, holding her gaze with his own.

Time seemed to stand still as she stared up at him, and she suddenly realised that he seemed to have lifted the careful barriers he usually kept between himself and the rest of the world.

Where once she'd had to look carefully to divine what he was thinking and feeling, now he was letting her see. It was the clear concern and compassion that she saw that made her doubts fade into oblivion.

He might not be in love with her—had never given her the slightest indication of it—but at least she could be certain that he didn't regard this marriage as some sort of personal sacrifice.

'Let's not keep the registrar waiting,' she murmured, and felt a smile on her face in answer to his own as an enormous weight disappeared off her shoulders.

'You may now kiss your bride,' the registrar said. Until that moment Abby had completely forgotten about that part of the ceremony. Forgotten—or deliberately put it out of her mind?

Whatever it was, she wasn't prepared for the way Ben turned her into his arms and gently touched his lips to hers.

She certainly wasn't prepared for the way that simple contact turned out to be anything but simple.

Her breath froze in her throat and her heart stumbled into a gallop, but none of that was enough to prevent her hearing the swiftly stifled moan she heard him make when their lips suddenly softened and clung.

'And a jolly good thing, too,' pronounced a clear Scottish accent, and they drew apart as though stung.

Abby hardly dared to do more than glance at Ben out of the corner of her eye during the signing of the register, but she was relieved to note that he seemed to be every bit as stunned as she by their first kiss.

'Now, then,' Celia said when they emerged into the bright sunshine of a glorious summer morning, 'I think you two ought to take yourselves off for a slap-up meal. After all, it's not every day you tie the knot.'

'Actually, I've booked a table for the three of us at that hotel facing Bedford Square.'

'Go on with you. You don't want me intruding on your celebrations!' she exclaimed forthrightly, but

Abby could tell that she was pleased to have been invited. 'I was very honoured that you asked me to be a witness—the only one you invited from the hospital, no less—but I think you need the rest of the day to yourselves.'

Abby added her voice to Ben's as he tried to change the older woman's mind, suddenly strangely shy of being alone with this man who was now her husband, but Celia was adamant.

She stayed only long enough to give Abby a swift hug and stretch up to plant an unexpected kiss on Ben's cheek before she bade them farewell.

'Be happy,' were her parting words and, true to her nature, they sounded more like an order than mere good wishes. Abby caught Ben's eye and they both laughed.

'Well, that tells us,' he said. He held out his elbow towards her again and led her round the side of the building towards his car.

The whole afternoon had a strangely surreal feeling as they lingered over their meal.

Outside the windows it was a glorious summer's day but they both had to admit that it felt very strange not to have to hurry back to work.

'It feels almost like playing truant,' Ben murmured as he ushered her back out to the street. 'I can't remember when I last spent a day when I didn't have half a dozen things to do and only enough time for three of them.'

They took a leisurely walk about the shops to buy some essentials to stock the kitchen for the week ahead, laughing when they discovered how many of their favourite brands coincided. It wasn't until Ben parked the car in the drive that Abby's nerves, which seemed to have disappeared during lunch, reappeared with a vengeance.

Ben had also grown silent, their conversation limited to the essentials as they unpacked their purchases. Finally, there was nothing else to do but make a cup of tea, and by that time the tension in the room was almost palpable.

When he reached across her to grab a couple of mugs and Abby nearly leapt out of her skin it seemed to be the last straw.

'For heaven's sake, Abby,' he exclaimed, thumping the mugs down on the work-surface and whirling to confront her. 'I thought you trusted me.'

'I—I do,' she stammered as her heart tried to leap into her throat. She knotted her fingers together to disguise their trembling but the gesture didn't escape him.

'It certainly doesn't look like it,' he said in disgust. 'You look as if you're afraid I'll rape you any minute.'

The ugly word fell into a hollow silence that grew to suffocating proportions as she stared at him, her face drained of colour.

'God, I'm sorry,' he muttered, obviously horrified by his slip of the tongue. 'I didn't mean—'

'It...it's all right, Ben,' she interrupted unsteadily, her hurt lessened by the self-condemnation she saw in his eyes. 'I know you didn't mean it like that. I know you wouldn't...' She shook her head wordlessly.

'Well, if you know, why are you shying away from me as if...' He flung his hands in the air when he couldn't immediately find the words he wanted. 'As if I might contaminate you if I get too close.'

Abby had a sudden vision of the kiss they'd shared at the end of the ceremony. She certainly hadn't been worried about any contamination then. Unfortunately, she couldn't quite find the courage to mention it.

'You haven't been frightened of me while you've been sharing my bed the last five nights, have you?' he demanded, and she caught a glimpse of uncertainty in his eyes that cut her to the quick.

'Oh, Ben, no. Not at all,' she hurried to reassure him.

'Then what's going on now? Is it the marriage? Are you regretting it already?'

'It's not that, it's... Oh, everything feels strange, and...and I didn't sleep very much last night for thinking about today, and my stomach's all upset...' Her outburst slowed to a trickle and stopped.

'Do you need a hug?' he asked, the sudden question shattering her precarious control.

'Yes, please,' she whispered, her eyes swimming with tears of gratitude when she saw the warmth and understanding in his face.

'So do I,' he admitted in a husky voice as he scooped her against himself and wrapped his arms tightly around her, burying his face in the soft curls of her freshly washed hair.

It was blissful, Abby thought as she leaned against him, knowing that he held her safe and secure. He was so big and warm and caring but so much more than that—he was the man she was falling in love with.

When she realised where her thoughts had taken her she tensed, but the more she thought about it the more she recognised the fact that she'd probably started falling in love with him the first time she'd met him.

The disaster with his twin had put a spoke in the wheel of progress, but their closeness over the last few days seemed to have accelerated the process.

'It'll work out, Abby,' Ben whispered as he tightened his arms even more, his warm breath teasing against her cheek and the side of her neck. 'Just give it time and it'll all work out.'

'It'll all work out,' Abby muttered with a scowl, as she wrapped her hands around a glass of water and prayed for the nausea to subside. 'Not if we never see each other, it won't.'

They'd been married for a week now and, if anything, she was seeing less of him than when they'd only worked together.

Oh, they lived in the same house and even slept in the same bed—after a fashion. Ben, however, stayed downstairs, listening to his guitar music, until sheer tiredness sent her to sleep, and when she woke up in the morning all she wanted to do was get to the bathroom as soon as possible.

So much for her fond dreams that their marriage of convenience might grow into a love match. If he never spent any time with her, how was he going to fall in love with her?

Abby had been hoping that these early days could develop into a belated courtship, and had visualised evenings spent together cooking and talking and eating—all the ways they could grow together.

The only bright spark was the fact that he'd enlisted Celia MacDonald's assistance in synchronising their shifts so that he was always available to provide her with transport on her way to and from work. She certainly couldn't complain that he wasn't taking his role as protector seriously.

Unfortunately, that seemed to have taken precedence over everything else, and she was beginning to despair of turning their relationship into anything more romantic.

A growing bustle at the other end of the department alerted her to the fact that there must be something important happening, and she put the glass of water aside.

'Thank goodness my squeamishness isn't affected by A and E gore,' she muttered as she walked swiftly in that direction, her heart giving a quick skip when she realised that the tall figure in front of her was Ben.

At least he couldn't disappear when the two of them were working together, especially when they did it so well.

She arrived just in time for the paramedic to give an overview of the patients his crew was bringing in.

'Car crash. Two injured—mother and baby. Father dead, probably on impact. Baby's very small, two or three months old. Thrown through windscreen at speed. Multiple injuries. We've put three IV lines in but she's losing blood faster than we can get it in. Mother has flail chest with multiple rib fractures, both legs are broken and there's a query on her pelvis. Complaining of headache and pain in her neck.'

As he recited his litany of horror they were already leaping into action, two teams hurrying their respective patients to opposite sides of the same large room where they clustered around to perform their particular tasks.

Abby only had time to notice that Ben had taken charge of the baby, her body looking like a pathetic broken doll on the blood-spattered trolley, before the woman in front of her commanded all her attention.

'My baby,' she moaned, the words muffled between the cervical collar protecting her neck and the mask covering the lower half of her face. The mask was to deliver one hundred per cent oxygen to counteract the effects of the flail chest. 'Where's Jilly? Where's Steven?'

'Is Steven your husband?' Abby demanded, clearly in an attempt to focus the woman's attention. She'd had to move away from her patient when the X-ray plates were being taken, her concern for her patient having to take second place to the safety of her own unborn child.

'Yes.' The woman's pain-filled eyes stared up at Abby, wide with fear 'Where is he? Is he all right? Where have they taken him?'

'Is Jilly your baby?' Abby asked, knowing there was no way her patient was in any condition to hear that her husband had died. 'How old is she?'

'Five months. She was premature. I was feeding her and—' Her face screwed up in a rictus of pain as one of the team tried very gently to cut away the last of her ruined clothes.

'Our first holiday since she came home,' she continued doggedly, almost as if she were using the words to block out what was happening to her. 'Going to Cornwall, back to our honeymoon hotel. Car came straight at us. Wrong side of the road. Big. Powerful. Going too fast.'

Abby could tell that in spite of the high concentration of oxygen she was receiving, the young woman was becoming increasingly breathless. From the tell-tale sounds she was picking up in the stethoscope it wasn't just because she was talking.

'I think we've got a pneumothorax,' she called, just as the monitor attached to the other little patient in the room emitted an ominous continuous tone.

Abby's head came up and she stared in horror at the flat green line marching across the monitor screen. Her eyes swept over the frantic activity around the tiny child, her body almost hidden behind the figures grouped around her as they fought to restart her heart.

She hadn't realised until then that Noah Kincaid had arrived in the room and had taken up a position opposite Ben to do what he could for the little girl.

When they heard Abby's warning that her patient might have a lung collapsing due to the repeated injury caused by the movement of the broken ribs, she saw Noah look up at Ben and nod in silent communication.

'Have we got any X-rays yet?' Ben demanded, as he listened to the ominous sounds inside the woman's badly injured chest, trying to determine whether the lung might have been punctured by one of the ribs. If the condition wasn't corrected swiftly, the build-up of air would collapse the lung, the level of carbon monoxide in her blood would rise and she could be in serious trouble.

'They've been taken and should be back in about two minutes.'

It was difficult to think clearly with the distraction of the staccato orders being given on the other side of the room. From the various electronic bleeps it was obvious that Noah was now trying to shock the baby's heart into activity, apparently without much success. With a total blood volume of about a teacup, the amount the infant was losing in spite of their best efforts must mean that there wasn't enough left to pump.

It was almost second nature to pass Ben the large-gauge through-the-needle catheter as soon as the second intercostal space had been wiped with an antibacterial swab.

'Where's Steven?' Abby's patient suddenly demanded in an increasingly breathless voice, as if she'd only just realised that no one had answered her question the first time. 'Why isn't he here?' she asked, her eyes staring around wildly when she realised that the collar round her neck was stopping her from seeing what was going on around her.

'He...he might be in the other room,' Abby suggested hurriedly, when it became obvious that Ben was going to have difficulty positioning the needle safely if she didn't calm down. 'If you lie very still, I promise I'll go and find out in just a minute.'

She held the woman's hand and her own breath as she watched Ben insert the tip of the needle along the upper border of the rib. She actually saw the pop as the needle reached the pleural space and then heard the air under pressure escaping through the catheter.

With the catheter advanced a couple of inches into the pleural cavity, Ben withdrew the needle, holding the catheter firmly until Abby could tape it safely into position.

The flail chest meant that the woman still couldn't take a deep breath, but at least she was no longer having to fight for every one.

It wasn't until she straightened that Abby noticed that there was no sound coming from the other side of the room, and with dread in her heart she looked across. The defeated look on Noah's face told her everything she needed to know, and when she met Ben's eyes she could tell that he was just as devastated.

'What's happened to my baby? What's the matter with Jilly?' demanded a frightened voice, the dread of premonition all too clear.

Abby squeezed her eyes tight shut for the space of

two seconds, but it wasn't enough to allow her to completely regain control of the urge to cry.

She hated losing any of their patients and the loss of babies had always seemed the most terrible, but this reaction was something else. Was it because she was carrying a child of her own that she was identifying so closely with the devastation this poor woman was about to suffer?

'Please. Somebody tell me. Where's Steven? What's happened to Jilly?'

With strength born of desperation she grabbed Abby's hand and clung, demanding an answer. She must have seen what the answer was in Abby's face because her mouth opened in a silent howl of denial as tears trickled from eyes empty of hope.

'I'm sorry,' Abby murmured helplessly, unable to comprehend fully the magnitude of the woman's loss. 'We did everything we could.'

'No.' There was bleak denial in the voice but somehow Abby knew that she didn't mean that her colleagues had failed in any way. 'Not Steven. Not Jilly. No. No. No...'

There were tears of sympathy in Abby's eyes but the sympathy swiftly turned to shock when the heart monitor attached to the woman's chest suddenly ceased its rhythmic bleep and issued an ominous single tone.

'She's arrested,' Ben snapped. Instantly Abby positioned herself on the opposite side to assist him with cardiopulmonary resuscitation.

The fact that the patient had broken ribs and there was a chance that she'd sustained neck injuries meant that their techniques had to be modified, but Abby automatically started rescue breathing after Ben had delivered his first set of fifteen compressions.

He swore viciously while she delivered two ventilations. 'There was no evidence of injury to the heart in spite of the flail chest. Get a tube down her quickly.'

He could have handed his exhausting task over to another member of staff but he seemed almost driven to perform the compressions himself, as if in this case he had a personal grudge against death.

For thirty minutes the whole team fought with every means at their disposal—physical, chemical and electrical—to get her heart started again, even resorting to opening up her chest as a last desperate measure in case a broken rib had damaged the heart.

When the silent organ was revealed, apparently unharmed but still totally unresponsive to any form of stimulation, Ben had to admit defeat, his head hanging down as he braced his bloody hands on the edge of the table.

'Ben, it wasn't your fault,' Abby whispered, her own heart aching with a desperate longing to put her arms around him. 'I think she just didn't want to live—not without her husband and child.'

Reaction didn't really set in until Abby had settled herself into bed that night. Ben had been very quiet on the journey home and his conversation during their meal had been sparse.

She'd hoped that for once he might have come upstairs with her so that they could have shared their thoughts, but when she heard the familiar sound of guitar music a single tear trickled down her cheek.

'No,' she muttered as she swiped it away angrily.

'I promised "for better, for worse" and today was definitely one of the worst.'

Abby knew that Ben had been devastated by his failure to keep the young woman alive, especially after losing her baby. He needed Abby and, heaven knew, she needed him.

She flounced out of the bed and, in the absence of a dressing-gown of her own, grabbed his towelling one off the hook behind the door before she marched barefoot down the stairs.

'Ben, this is stupid,' she announced as she pushed the door open and stepped into the sitting room. 'We need to talk about this…'

She'd been so concerned with finding the right words to say that she hadn't noticed the music had stopped until she saw him sitting there with a guitar balanced across his lap.

'Ben?' She stood, looking uncertainly from his face to the instrument and back again as she put the details together. 'Has that been *you* playing every evening?' she whispered at last, the memory of the liquid perfection that had wrapped itself around her each night to send her to sleep somehow even more precious now that she knew who had been creating it.

'It's just a hobby,' he murmured dismissively, his eyes fixed on the rich glow of the elegant instrument as he prepared to set it aside.

'Just a hobby!' she exclaimed in amazement, her feet carrying her over to him in a rush. 'But you play beautifully. What was the name of that piece? I've never heard it before.'

'It hasn't really got a name,' he said, and something in his response told her there was more to it than that.

'Is that because you haven't given it a name yet?' she challenged softly. 'You did write it, didn't you?'

He shrugged and she could tell from the sweep of colour across his face that he was reticent about this hidden talent of his.

'Will you play it for me? Please?' she begged when he began to shake his head. She was certain suddenly that this could be an important turning point for the two of them. 'It's such a soothing tune, and after a day like today I need to be soothed—we both do.'

She sank cross-legged to the floor and stared expectantly up at him as though sure that he would comply. Only *she* knew that the hands cradled together in her lap hid tightly crossed fingers.

For long moments there was a deep, breathless silence in the room and even when he put the guitar back on his knee she wasn't absolutely certain that he would play for her. It wasn't until the first plangent notes twined themselves around her senses that she dared to release the breath she'd been holding.

At first her eyes were drawn to the way his long fingers caressed the instrument, their lean strength deceptive as he brought faultless harmonies from the strings.

Gradually her attention widened until her gaze was drawn up to his face where, to her surprise, she found that he was also watching her.

Once their eyes met it was impossible to look away, and as the plaintive, passionate tune began to work its magic on her it seemed as if it drew all her emotions closer and closer to the surface. By the time the final chord faded her tears were spilling over and trickling down her cheeks.

'Ah, Abby, don't,' Ben murmured, putting the instrument aside and capturing her hands. His eyes were suspiciously bright too, and she knew that he'd been just as deeply moved as she was.

'Please, Ben,' she whispered, not quite certain what she was asking for other than the fact that she needed to be close to him.

'What do you want?' He stood up and helped her to her feet, placing one arm around her shoulders and leading her to the bottom of the stairs when she shook her head dumbly. 'You're tired,' he pronounced solicitously, and paused to brush away her tears with gentle fingers. 'Can I get you anything before you go to bed?'

'Nothing.' She shook her head, then took her courage in both hands as she looked straight up into his eyes. 'Please, will you come up with me, Ben? I really need you to be there tonight.'

There was a flicker of something stormy in his expression but he'd got it back under control before she was able to identify it.

He was silent for so long that she was sure he was going to refuse. Then he gave a single nod and began to climb the stairs with her.

There was a dream-like quality to the silence in the room as she shed his dressing-gown and slid back under the covers, all the while knowing that the sounds going on behind her meant that he was taking off his clothes, ready to join her in the bed.

A foolish shyness stopped her looking towards him and she kept her eyes fixed on his very masculine, plain, forest-green curtains until the mattress dipped, telling her that the body she was longing to admire was safely under cover.

The accidental brush of his arm against her told her that he was wearing little, if anything. She could feel the heat in her cheeks that told her she was blushing like a schoolgirl, but there were more important things at stake than her sensibilities. Ben had been devastated by the double tragedy today, and although he would probably deny to his last breath that he wanted to be pampered she had a strong feeling that it was just what he needed.

'Ben?' she whispered, the coward in her making her wait until he'd switched off the light before she dared to speak. 'Will you hold me...please?'

She didn't know whether the rumble she heard was his assent or a groan, but she barely suppressed a groan of her own when he hauled her tightly against him, his arms holding her so close that their hearts seemed to beat in unison.

It was long, blissful moments later that, in spite of her nervousness at his sheer naked size, the feeling of warmth and security surrounding her allowed her to relax.

He was so still and silent beside her that she grew bold enough to smooth her hand over the rough silk of his hair, but it wasn't until he seemed to have ignored her overture that she realised he'd fallen asleep in her arms.

She'd wondered if he'd want to talk and had been perfectly willing to listen. This was even better, she thought, smiling happily as she herself began to drift off.

CHAPTER NINE

ABBY opened her eyes slowly and groaned.

It was the first time since their marriage that she and Ben had gone to bed together and woken up together, but last night they'd fallen asleep almost as soon as he'd put his arms around her. She wasn't going to be able to enjoy it this morning either because if she moved more than an eyelash she was going to have to run to be sick.

Ever since morning sickness had struck, she'd tried everything—sipping fizzy glucose drinks, nibbling dry biscuits—all to no avail.

She lay perfectly still and tried breathing slowly to put off the evil moment just long enough to savour the feeling of his long, powerful body wrapped sleepily around hers.

If the peaceful expression on his face was anything to go by he'd needed a night of uninterrupted sleep, too, and she wasn't surprised that in his arms the nightmare had stayed away.

She began to catalogue the way that even in sleep he held her tightly against him. One of his thighs was thrown possessively across hers, but the sharp twist of arousal that caused in the pit of her stomach was too much for her system to cope with.

'Uh-oh,' she muttered through clenched teeth, as she tried to fight her way out of his hold and out of the bedclothes without losing her precarious control.

She was vaguely aware of him saying her name in

a puzzled voice as she dived headlong towards the toilet, but there wasn't time to dwell on the regret that she hadn't been able to stay to watch him wake.

In spite of a good night's sleep, work that day felt like she was pushing a boulder up a steep hill. The baby inside her was probably less than an inch long but the hormonal tidal wave it caused in her body was leaving her exhausted.

On top of that it was a niggling sort of day. The waiting area was filled with a multitude of minor problems, most of which should really have been dealt with at a GP's surgery.

What few, more urgent cases there were seemed to be taken care of by other members of staff so that time hung heavily on her hands.

If she'd been able to spend some of that time with Ben she'd have thought it well spent, but he seemed to be the only one constantly in demand.

It was the same when she reached the end of her shift, her own duties ending while he was still in the middle of trying to stabilise a patient with suspected cardiac arrest ready to transfer him up to intensive care.

'I could be another hour yet,' he warned her, when he realised that she was patiently waiting to go home, nearly asleep on her feet. 'Why not grab my keys and drive yourself home? I can always take a taxi.'

There was some good-natured ribbing from the other staff in the room that he was making a mistake to let her get her hands on the keys to his car.

'Bad move, Ben. You should start as you mean to go on,' advised the hovering anaesthetist, just one of the people who had teased the pair of them unmercifully about their sudden marriage.

Ben ignored him and, holding his hands up out of the way, angled his hip towards Abby so that she could help herself to his keys.

The ribbing started again when the unexpected intimacy of the position as she delved into the depths of his trouser pocket made her fumble, and they teased her that she was taking far too long just to be looking for his keys.

'Abby,' Ben called softly, as she whirled away with her face flaming, the keys clenched tightly enough in her hand to score her palms.

'Yes?' She turned back, expecting some special instruction about driving the car or when to expect him, and was startled when he angled his head and gave her a swift kiss.

'Drive carefully. See you soon,' he murmured while she was still trying to calm her heartbeat and catch her breath. Then he gave her a wicked private wink that promised more of the same.

She was still wearing a smile of besotted anticipation when she heard the knock on the door an hour later—an hour in which every nerve had been singing as she wondered exactly what the expression in his eyes had meant as he'd held her gaze for several heated seconds.

Did it mean that her hopes were going to come true? Would tonight be the night when they finally made their marriage something more than a convenience?

'No keys,' she muttered as she hurried to the door to let him in, realising that they must have been on the same bunch that she'd fished out of his pocket. Her hand still seemed to hold the memory of the amazing heat of his body, and she felt a response deep inside her as she reached out for the latch and saw the outline of Ben's dark head through the ornate stained-glass panel set in the door.

'That didn't take as long as you thought,' she said as she opened the door, embarrassed by the husky tone in her voice.

'Too bloody long. But I've found you now,' snarled the voice from her nightmares. He pushed her aside and slammed the door behind him so hard that part of the fragile glass design shattered and fell out onto the front door step.

'Ben,' she breathed, her heart in her mouth as she looked at all-too-familiar features. Only this wasn't Ben, was it? She knew the difference now—could see that the similarities were all on the surface.

'You're *not* Ben,' she accused flatly, straightening away from the wall he'd flung her against. She sent up a mental prayer that Ben—*her* Ben—was on his way home, then she squared her shoulders, ignoring the throbbing ache that signalled the formation of yet another bruise at this man's hands. 'I don't know why I ever thought you were.'

'Ah, but I *am* Ben,' he contradicted smoothly. 'Only I'm Benjamin and he's Benedict.' He laughed without a trace of humour, his twisted expression a travesty of the good-natured man she loved. 'Clever joke our dear departed mother played, wasn't it—giving identical twins nearly identical names? Unfortunately, nothing else was identical.'

Abby stayed silent while he fired his bitterness at her like bullets.

Her independent spirit made her want to demand that he left, but the instinct of self-preservation told her she daren't do anything to goad him into an outburst of violence. Last time had been bad enough but this time it would be her baby at risk, not just herself.

Almost involuntarily her hand crept down to hover protectively over that fragile new life as she realised how much it had come to mean to her—in spite of its beginnings.

'He got everything,' Ben continued savagely. 'She sold him to wealthy people who adopted him and handed everything to him on a plate—a home, schooling, career, women falling all over themselves to get at him. And what did I get? Nothing.'

'But it wasn't like that.' Abby was stung into argument before she realised she was going to speak, and once she'd started there seemed no reason she shouldn't continue. She knew that Ben would be here soon and she had absolute faith that he wouldn't let anything awful happen to her again.

She'd had enough of being terrorised and intimidated by this bully, and it was time that he got a few of his facts straight.

'If you'd bothered to do any checking, you'd know that his mother's an invalid with a heart problem and his father's an ordinary working man. Ben's had to work hard for everything he's got—in case you hadn't realised it, money won't buy you qualifications as a doctor. Only sheer hard graft does that.'

'And the women?' he sneered, apparently dismissing her defence of the man she loved as irrelevant. 'You can't tell me you'd be so keen to lift your skirt for him if he wasn't a doctor. You were keen enough to go out with me when you thought I was him.'

'I've never lifted my skirt for *anybody*, doctor or not,' she said hotly, the anger she'd been suppressing inside her ever since this man had attacked her suddenly boiling to the surface. 'It was too special to me. I wanted to...to save myself...to wait for my wedding night...but *you* took that away from me.'

'What's the odds?' he demanded with oily insinuation, not a hint of remorse in his voice. 'He married you anyway so you got what you were angling for. Tell me, are we identical all over?'

Abby clenched her teeth tightly and refused to dignify the question with an answer. Instead, she fired one of her own at him.

'Tell me why,' she demanded. For the sake of her own peace of mind she had to know. 'Why did you pick on me and why did you attack me?'

'I asked you out because I wanted to see if I could fool everyone,' he said arrogantly. 'I'd been watching him for weeks, ever since I saw that picture in the paper when he moved here. I saw the way the two of you were looking sideways at each other and suddenly I wanted to prove that I could pull it off.'

Abby was uncomfortable at the idea that anyone had been watching her and embarrassed that they'd noticed her attraction towards Ben. She'd thought she'd hidden it so well. But this wasn't the time to allow her thoughts to sidetrack her.

'OK, that explains why you asked me out the first time, but what about the rest?'

He was silent for a moment and didn't seem to want to meet her eyes, then the words exploded from him in renewed anger.

'I was attracted to you. OK? You were nice and sweet and gentle, and everything I'd never had. But all you wanted was *him*. All you ever wanted to talk about was the work you'd done together and the people you both knew. It was all *his* life and I was on the outside...always on the outside, looking in at what everybody else had.'

The anger in his words wasn't feigned. It obviously overflowed from a deep well of unhappiness and deprivation stretching right back to his childhood.

But that still didn't give him the right to attack her, to subject her to such a violation. *Nothing* gave a man the right to do that.

'But...if you liked me, why did you...?' The tears were welling up and stopped her from speaking, but she wasn't certain who she was crying for—herself, for inadvertently coming between the two of them and ending up as the unwitting victim, or for the man in front of her, once as full of potential as his twin but now reduced to this...

'Dammit, it was *your* fault,' he snarled, as defensive as a cornered wolf. 'You were going out with me and talking with me but you thought I was him. That night, on your doorstep, I wanted to tell you. I wanted you to know it was me, but you started talking about your fancy friends at the hospital wanting to know who you were going out with, and weren't they going to get a surprise when they found out it was me.'

He gave another of those dreadful hollow laughs and it sent a shiver up her spine.

'Suddenly I knew what a waste of time it had all been. You didn't want me. You wanted him and I could never compete.'

His mouth twisted again and Abby began to wonder if he'd lose control before Ben arrived.

Hurry, Ben, please, hurry, she thought, her eyes straying to the telephone cord just inside the sitting room as she wondered if she'd have a chance to use it.

'Do you know,' he continued, 'how good it was to see him going through the mill for a change when the police picked him up? I may not have his fancy qualifications but I've heard enough to know they'd match the DNA.' He glared at her. 'You were supposed to identify him and put him away, but what did you do? Crawled into bed with him instead and then got him to marry you. It wasn't supposed to *be* that way. You were supposed to give him a taste of what it's been like to be me—'

A single sudden sound behind him was all the warning he had before the arm Abby had seen reaching stealthily through the broken glass had released the catch and the door was flung open behind him.

'Ben!' Abby gasped. He stood framed in the doorway, his expression thunderous as he raked her from head to foot as though examining her for injury. Her heart was beating too fast for her to say anything further, a frantic combination of pleasure at seeing him and fear for his safety.

'Welcome, brother, dear,' the man she loved said ironically as he held up his mobile phone. 'I hope you won't mind that I took the liberty of inviting a few friends to this unexpected reunion.'

'Friends?' An animal wariness entered Benjamin's eyes. Seeing them together for the first time, Abby marvelled that she'd ever mistaken one for the other. Benedict cocked his head, drawing their attention to the approaching sound of sirens.

'All three emergency services—fire, police and ambulance. I wasn't taking any chances that you'd hurt Abby again. You've already caused her enough pain.'

With a vicious stream of curses Benjamin glared from one to the other, then knocked his brother aside as he raced out of the house.

Twilight was darkening towards night as he burst out of the gateway, and in the confusion of flashing lights and shadows Abby lost sight of him. Part of her couldn't help being sorry for him, in spite of the fact that fear-induced adrenaline was still flooding through her body, and she half wished that he could evade capture. Being one of identical twins, surely he was enough like her husband that he was good at heart?

She was standing just inside the hallway, her knees quivering with a combination of fear and relief, when she heard the sudden screech of brakes and a terrible thump—then the ominous silence that followed them.

'Oh, God, no,' she heard Ben groan, as he took off at a run.

Abby followed, dreading what she was going to see and what it would do to Ben.

By the time she reached the cluster of people grouped around the front of a police car Ben was already issuing orders, enlisting the help of the officers so that he could assess his brother's injuries.

'I need light,' he snapped, and within seconds car headlights had been switched on to bathe the scene in brilliance. 'Clear the way for the ambulance,' he directed, without looking up from his task, as he checked his brother's airway, breathing and circulation. 'Tell them they'll need to bring a backboard.'

For long moments Abby stood staring down at the crumpled figure in front of her, not knowing whether to hope that he couldn't be a threat to her any more. Then the memory of the little he'd told her about his childhood flashed into her mind and stirred her compassion again.

She saw Ben tearing at the buttons on the bloodied shirt to reveal his brother's chest, and years of training took over.

'What can I do?' she demanded as she knelt beside Ben in the middle of the road.

'Stay by his head. He's unconscious at the moment but you need to hold his neck still until we get a collar on him. And watch his breathing.'

Somewhere in the background she heard a man muttering over and over, 'I couldn't avoid him. He tripped and I couldn't avoid him.' Her concentration, however, was fixed on the remarkably familiar face in front of her.

Until the ambulance arrived with a cervical collar she'd have to make sure that any damage done to his neck wasn't made worse by moving him around, and the easiest way to do that was to brace his head with a hand on either side.

Out of the corner of her eyes she could see Ben, methodically working his way down his twin's body to check for injuries. She could only guess from his increasingly grim expression that there were several.

The arrival of the paramedic was a relief and it wasn't until her task had been taken over that she realised she'd been holding the face of her attacker without a single qualm, all her emotion reserved for Ben and what he was going through.

Within minutes of Ben climbing into the ambulance to travel with his brother to the hospital, Abby had locked up the house and was following them.

She wasn't in uniform, but that didn't stop her hurrying through the department to catch up with Ben just as his brother regained consciousness.

'Leave me alone,' he was snarling up at Ben, their faces remarkably similar in spite of their different expressions. 'If I'm going to snuff it then at least it'll stop me having to do time. If she's laid charges against me they're going to throw the book at me anyway.'

Abby could see avid curiosity on the faces of the rest of the team but she had to give them points for carrying on with their jobs regardless.

While his injured brother was arguing his clothes were being cut away and X-rays taken, blood samples were drawn up for cross-matching and monitor leads were attached.

Feeling like a ghoulish spectator at some sort of nightmare ritual, Abby stood at the far side of the room. She wasn't on duty, any more than Ben was, but she was gripped by the feeling that she had to be there.

One of the monitors gave a warning shriek that his blood pressure was dropping far too low and her attention sharpened, her eyes going swiftly from one display to another with a dreadful sense of impending disaster.

'He's arrested!' somebody said, as several monitors joined in the cacophony.

'No!' shouted Ben, and Abby knew she wasn't the only one who heard the agony in his voice.

Seemingly in slow motion she saw the way he glared at the rest of the staff, as if daring them to lose this patient, then the fight began.

It was a strange replay of the events just a few hours ago when he'd fought to resuscitate the young mother after losing her tiny baby.

The difference came when the chest cavity was opened to reveal the damage done by a broken rib. Abby could imagine, from what they were saying and what she'd seen in the past, how the punctured heart would be spurting blood into the chest cavity with each vital thrust as they tried to keep the circulation going.

'I've got it,' Ben snapped. She saw him reach a gloved hand in swiftly to block the wound. 'Phone Theatre and tell them we're on our way up.'

Abby was still there, leaning against the wall, when Celia MacDonald bustled by. The room had been cleared and returned to its usual pristine order while she stood there but she'd hardly noticed, her thoughts centred totally on the events of the last couple of hours.

'Mercy, child, what are you doing in here?' the senior sister scolded, and ushered her through to her office. 'You look as if you could do with a dram of whisky to put some colour in your cheeks. Unfortunately I can only offer you tea or coffee.'

'Tea, please,' she murmured distractedly, for once her thoughts too occupied with what was going on upstairs to allow her to react to the thought of coffee.

'They do look remarkably alike,' the older woman said, as she sat beside Abby with a cup of her own. The seemingly innocuous comment was enough to open the floodgates.

'They didn't even know the other existed, not until just a few weeks ago. Apparently, their mother gave Ben up to be adopted...' She paused and laughed wearily when she heard what she'd said. 'Can you believe it? They're both called Ben. And then, before they even have a chance to get to know each other...' She shook her head wildly, not wanting to contemplate what it would do to Ben if his brother didn't survive.

'Shh, lassie, shh,' Big Mac soothed. 'Don't borrow trouble. It'll all turn out the way it's meant to in the end.'

'I hope you're right, Sister,' said a voice in the doorway. 'At least for the moment he's in with a fighting chance.'

'He's still alive?' Abby demanded, swaying on her feet when she leapt up too quickly.

'Not out of surgery yet,' Ben said, moving swiftly to grab her elbow to steady her. To Abby's delight he didn't release her but wrapped his arm round her to hold her by his side while he finished his report.

'Orthopaedics are working on him. They've got to pin his leg and put it into traction to align the broken ends, and his ribs are a bit of a jigsaw puzzle, but Cardiology are optimistic that they've patched up all the leaks.'

'Well, in that case, I think it's time the two of you went home,' Celia MacDonald pronounced firmly. 'Tomorrow morning will be quite soon enough to see your faces around here. In fact, I think it would be a fine idea if the two of you had the day off.'

Some private communication passed between her superior and the man at her side but Abby wasn't quick enough to catch it. She did see the broad wink Big Mac sent her husband's way when he suggested the older woman notified the powers-that-be about the timetable changes, but suddenly she was too exhausted to care.

The journey back home was a blur after Ben's teasing comment about her haphazard parking, and she could hardly put one foot in front of the other as she made her way up the stairs, leaving him to check the temporary repair made to the front door.

She stood by the bed for several minutes, trying to remember what she was supposed to be doing.

'Come on, sleepyhead,' he chided as he reached for the first of the buttons on the front of her shirt and slid it through the hole. She hardly noticed that she was standing naked before him until he pulled her T-shirt nightdress over her head and she caught a brief glimpse of a strange heat in his eyes.

'Bathroom?' he suggested, and pointed her in the right direction. He collected her again when she re-emerged, and patiently urged her under the covers.

'You, too,' Abby muttered, grabbing at his hand and holding on tightly, knowing she needed to feel him close to her.

'As soon as I've taken my clothes off,' he promised, and even with her eyes closed she could tell he was smiling.

The next thing she knew was when she woke up in the darkness to feel Ben's arms around her. Feeling the tension in the body beside her, she knew that he was awake, too.

'Ben?' she whispered, wondering what direction his thoughts had taken.

'I'm sorry, didn't mean to wake you,' he murmured, his voice a soft rumble in the quiet room and a deeper one through the wall of his chest under her ear.

'I'm sorry I fell asleep like that,' she countered. 'I just couldn't keep my eyes open.'

He was silent for a moment before he spoke again.

'Every time I close mine I see him,' he admitted quietly. 'It's the first time I've ever come face to face with my brother and I end up with his heart in my hand.'

Even without being able to see his expression, Abby could hear the mixture of awe and distress in his voice.

'Do you want to ring through to Intensive Care to see how he's doing?' she suggested quietly. In spite of what his twin had done to her, she needed to know the answer and could only guess how much stronger the feeling must be for him.

He reached out to turn on the light and she watched his expression as he dialled. The relief she saw there when he got through told her that the news was good.

'It looks like he's going to make it,' he reported as he slid back down beside her, wrapping his arms around her as though the action had become completely automatic.

Abby had been enjoying looking at him, savouring the way the soft light outlined the shape of the muscles that went to make up his shoulders and chest, the taut ligaments in his fingers and wrist as he held the phone and his lean profile and rumpled hair.

She liked the feel of him under the covers with her, their bodies touching all the way from shoulder to ankle—almost as if they were two halves of a whole.

'You know, this wasn't quite how I was hoping this evening would go,' he commented in a musing sort of way.

'Hardly,' she said with a chuckle, glad to hear that the tension had largely disappeared from his voice and only too willing to put her own fear behind her. 'What *did* you have in mind?'

'Well, I was going to suggest getting in a take-away meal to save both of us from kitchen duties, and then

I was going to suggest that we both needed an early night.'

Abby's heart sank a little at his prosaic answer. It wasn't quite what she'd been expecting, but she supposed he was right, really. They had been very short of sleep for some time now.

'Well, Big Mac's arranged for us both to have the day off tomorrow,' she reminded him, hoping that her disappointment didn't show. After that teasing kiss she'd been so certain that there'd been an element of promise in his wicked wink. It must have been wishful thinking. 'At least we'll be able to have a lie-in and catch up on some sleep.'

'We could,' he agreed quietly, but there was something slightly different in his tone that made her look up at him. 'On the other hand, I was rather hoping that we could...talk.'

As she watched him she could see the skin over his cheek-bones darken, and when his eyes met hers there was that same intent expression in them that she'd glimpsed several times before. This time he made no attempt to hide it, deliberately holding her gaze for several long seconds.

'Wh-what did you want to...talk about?' she murmured, all too conscious of her body reacting to the growing flare of heat in his eyes.

Her nipples began to tighten against the soft cotton of her T-shirt and her breasts grew heavy as the strange ache deep inside her made her want to move even closer to him.

'I...I can't remember,' he muttered distractedly. She felt an answering flare of heat in her own cheeks when she saw that his eyes were now fixed on the pointed evidence of her growing arousal. 'All I can think about is the fact that I'm going to go crazy, lying next to you in bed like this.'

Abby drew in a deep breath for courage. At the back of her mind there still lurked an atavistic fear of putting herself in a position of vulnerability with someone so much bigger and stronger, but that trepidation was warring with her growing love for him.

In the end her instinctive knowledge that she could trust him not to hurt her meant that love had to win.

'Is there anything I can do to help?' she whispered, her heart beating a frantic tattoo. She flicked the tip of her tongue over suddenly parched lips. 'I...I wouldn't want to be responsible for your insanity if there was something I could do to prevent—'

She squeaked in surprise as he suddenly tightened his arms around her and rolled onto his back, leaving her draped across his evidently aroused body and gazing down at him wide-eyed.

'Then kiss me, Abby,' he growled as he speared long fingers through the shimmering tumble of her hair to cradle her head in gentle hands. 'If you want to save my sanity, kiss me.'

CHAPTER TEN

ABBY glanced across at the alarm clock and smiled. Ten o'clock already and no morning sickness. Perhaps her body hadn't realised the time—it certainly hadn't had very much sleep last night.

She heard a clatter drifting up from the kitchen as Ben gathered the ingredients to bring her breakfast in bed, and stretched lazily.

'I'm going to pamper you,' he'd promised between kisses that had threatened to grow out of control in spite of the number of times they'd made love during the night.

Abby winced as a muscle pulled at the side of her stomach, and she felt the heat of a blush cover her from her breasts right up to her hairline. They'd certainly done a few things that used muscles she hadn't discovered before, had never even imagined...

She sighed when she remembered how gentle Ben had been, how considerate of the fact that she might still be traumatised by his brother's attack.

Once he'd been certain that it was what she wanted he'd been patience itself, arousing her with kisses and touches and teaching her how to arouse him until suddenly a conflagration had ignited between them. Then there'd been no difference between teacher and pupil as they'd gone up in flames together.

Abby had cried a little, regretting that it hadn't been her first experience of sex, but when Ben had held her close and comforted her it hadn't been long before the flames had risen again and her regrets had burned away to ashes.

It had been the same throughout the night, their desires no sooner satisfied than one had looked at or brushed against the other and they'd been rekindled, burning higher and hotter until at last they'd collapsed into slumber.

The sound of approaching footsteps was enough to start the spiral tightening inside her again. She'd never realised how much sensuality there was inside her until he'd shown her. Once she might have tried to hide her reaction to him, but now that she knew it excited him too...

'Don't look at me like that until I've had something to eat,' Ben grumbled with an attempt at sternness. 'You're going to wear me away to a frazzle.'

'And this is the man who begged me to save him from insanity. The ingratitude of it!' she retorted, loving the teasing smile he threw her way.

She wriggled up the bed with just a sheet to preserve some measure of decorum, and twisted to settle the pillow at her back.

'Ouch,' she squeaked, and pressed a hand over the muscle that was complaining again.

'Sore?' he demanded with a concerned frown, the glass of apple juice she'd requested suspended in mid-air.

'I think I might have pulled a muscle or something,' she said, noticing that the pain was slower to subside this time. 'Otherwise, I've never felt better in my life.'

'You're sure? No regrets?' he prompted, shedding his dressing-gown and sliding under the covers again. His naked thigh settled with new familiarity against hers.

'How could I?' she countered carefully, knowing in her heart of hearts that she did have just one—the regret that no matter how often or how well they'd *made* love to each other he'd never *said* the word.

She reached across for a piece of toast and the pain hit her again, stronger than ever. She gritted her teeth but still couldn't hold back a cry.

'What is it, Abby? What's the matter?' The worry in Ben's voice drew her out of her concentration on the discomfort.

'I don't know. I think we might have been a little over-ambitious last night, considering my amateur status,' she said, trying to make light of it. 'The complaints department seems to be open for business this morning.'

'Dammit, I'm sorry,' Ben said, depositing the tray on the floor with a clatter and turning back to her. 'Where does it hurt, Abby?'

'I'm sure I've only pulled a muscle,' she said with a reassuring smile, 'but I'm happy to show you where if you want to play doctors and nurses. You could kiss it better.'

She started to slide down the bed, putting on what she hoped was a seductive smile, when the pain hit again, but this time it was different, almost explosive, and it seemed to grow and grow. Then she felt a strange, oozing warmth and fear gripped her with vicious talons.

'Ben, help me,' she whispered, her voice almost frozen in her throat as she grabbed for his arm. 'I think I'm losing the baby.'

Everything descended into confusion once Ben had phoned for an ambulance. He was trying to help her into his dressing-gown without causing her any more pain, at the same time scrambling into some clothes himself.

Abby was barely conscious of what was going on around her, the pain so fierce now that it blotted out everything but Ben's litany of apologies.

'Oh, Abby, I'm so sorry. It's all my fault,' he murmured, as he knelt beside the bed and gripped her hand. 'If I hadn't been so impatient, so greedy... Please, God, don't let her lose the baby. Oh, Abby, please forgive me...'

By the time the ambulancemen arrived to rush her to St Augustine's the pain was so great that the Entonox barely seemed to touch it.

The only things she was really conscious of were the sound of Ben's voice and the warm strength of his grip. They kept her focused, but even as she heard the misplaced misery and guilt in his voice there was no way she could form the words to absolve him.

Abby was vaguely aware of their arrival at the emergency entrance and Ben's insistence that she should be transferred straight up to Obstetrics and Gynaecology. After that she remembered nothing.

'So pale,' Ben whispered, as he devoured Abby's sleeping face with his eyes, not daring to touch her in case he woke her.

Her hair was spread out across the pillow in silver-gilt spirals, just the way it had been last night in his bed—the way it had been for countless nights before, when he'd dreamed about her and imagined her there.

And last night she'd made every dream come true and she'd done it willingly, with laughter and joyous abandon and an enthusiasm he'd never dared to hope for.

And then this.

He shuddered when he remembered how guilty he'd felt when he'd thought he'd caused her to lose the baby. It had been almost a relief to find out it had been an ectopic pregnancy. The embryo had implanted itself in Abby's Fallopian tube, growing until it had finally burst the walls of its prison.

'I nearly lost you,' he murmured, fear gripping him again when he remembered exactly how close she'd come to bleeding to death in front of him. 'So much blood…' To replace it they'd had to push it into her so fast that she'd probably have a monumental headache when she woke up.

He closed his eyes and tried to shut out the thoughts that followed, but they wouldn't stay away. She was going to wake up and he'd have to tell her that it had been an ectopic pregnancy. He was going to have to tell her that the surgeon had been unable to repair her ruptured Fallopian tube and had removed the ovary on that side to increase her chances of a normal pregnancy next time.

Next time.

He only had to think of it and he had to swallow the bile that rose in his throat, wondering who the father of that child would be—knowing it couldn't be himself.

He'd been falling in love with her ever since he'd first joined the staff at St Augustine's but it had only been her misfortune that had persuaded her to marry him. Now that she'd lost the baby there'd be no reason for her to stay—no leverage he could use to persuade her.

He'd just have to face it—in spite of the most magical night of his life, she hadn't once told him she loved him.

Abby opened heavy eyelids just a crack and found herself in a high hospital bed with an IV line running blood into her arm. What had happened to her? Her brain was too fuzzy to think properly.

Her mouth was dry, she had the mother and father of all headaches and her stomach felt as if it had been ripped open with a rusty knife.

'Hello?' She tried to call, her eyes closing with the effort, but it only emerged as a hoarse croak, the sound echoing briefly in the confines of the single room in which she'd been placed.

'Abby?'

Ben's husky voice made her force her eyes open wide and there he was, a worried frown furrowing his forehead as he leant over her.

'How are you feeling?' he demanded urgently.

He didn't look as if he'd slept in days. There were dark circles under his eyes and his skin was drawn too tightly over the bones of his face.

'Thirsty,' she whispered, and he gave her just enough water to wet her mouth.

Even though he put a strong arm around her to lift her, the effort of holding her head up intensified the pain in her belly and she groaned. 'It hurts,' she breathed, and suddenly she remembered everything that had happened.

'Oh, Ben. The baby,' she moaned weakly, fumbling to find his hand and clinging to it with unexpected strength. 'What happened to the baby?'

'It was ectopic,' he said gruffly, and she saw in his eyes a reflection of the pain that she was feeling. 'It had implanted in the Fallopian tube and when it ruptured...' He shook his head and she saw him swallow before he could continue. 'It happened so fast and you were losing so much blood. We only just got you here in time.'

She was silent for a long time before she spoke again, but eventually she had her muddled thoughts in order. In spite of the pain in her heart—rivalling the one in her belly—she knew what she had to do.

'How long will I have to stay here?' she whispered, bleakly, as she drew her hand away from his and tried to close him out by shutting her eyes. 'When can I go home?'

'But this *is* your home,' Ben declared for the umpteenth time as he paced backwards and forwards in his sitting room. 'We're married and—'

'That can soon be changed,' Abby said quietly, hearing how emotionless and flat her voice sounded but unable to summon up the energy to care. It was what she'd decided in the hospital and nothing had happened to change her mind.

'We both know that the only reasons you married me were because of the baby and to keep me safe. Neither of those reasons is valid any more so there's no reason why you should be tied to the arrangement.'

If she hadn't known better, she might almost imagine that her words had hurt him—but that was ridiculous. He was such a trustworthy man with such a strong sense of responsibility that there was no way he would tell her that he wanted to be set free. So it was up to her to do it for him. She could never live with herself if she had him tied to a loveless marriage.

'But where will you go?' he demanded, running his

fingers through his hair and leaving it stuck up at all angles.

'Back to my flat, of course,' she said, as if the answer was obvious. She ignored the silly urge to smooth his hair down again.

'You can't!' he exclaimed. 'It still hasn't been cleared out and there isn't a stick of furniture in the place worth having.'

'Spit and polish and a quick shopping trip will solve that,' she pointed out, careful not to let him see that she had no idea where she was going to get the energy from. What mattered most was that she wouldn't have to stay here with him, tantalised by the very thing she couldn't have.

'For heaven's sake, woman, will you talk sense?' he demanded, clearly at the end of his tether. 'You're in no fit state to go heaving things around and won't be for weeks yet. At least let me go there today and get rid of the mess for you. I can probably find a cleaning firm to do the rest, if not today then probably tomorrow.'

Abby subsided, knowing that he was right. It was one thing to want to get away from the temptation of staying with him but it was another entirely to risk doing herself some permanent damage before she'd healed.

'All right,' she agreed, and leaned back weakly in the chair when he left the room, horrified by how much energy it had taken just to argue with him. How long was it going to take before she was fit to go back to work?

'One last thing before I go,' he said half an hour later, when he'd changed into an old pair of threadbare jeans and collected plastic bags and boxes ready to begin his self-imposed task.

He grabbed a piece of paper off the bookcase beside the telephone and moved the instrument over beside her before he began to dial.

It seemed to be an inordinately long number but finally she heard it ring and then a voice answered at the other end.

'Here,' he said, giving the receiver to her. Then he stepped back towards the door as if he couldn't wait to leave. 'I promised her you'd be in contact.'

'Hello?' Abby said, wondering who was on the other end.

'Abby, darling, are you all right? Why didn't you let us know you needed us?' said a familiar voice, unchanged by the thousands of miles between them.

'Mum?' Abby said, utter disbelief giving a quiver to the word. 'Oh, Mum, is that really you?' She didn't know whether to laugh or cry.

She suddenly remembered that she ought to thank Ben for doing this for her, but when she looked over her shoulder he was already out of sight. Sadly, she realised that he seemed to be in an awful hurry to sort her flat out so that he could finally get her out of his life.

'Oh, Mum, I wish you were here,' she wailed, needing the comfort of a consoling hug. 'I've made such a mess of everything.'

Ben had reached the car with his armful of paraphernalia before he realised that he must have left the keys on the bookcase when he'd picked up the telephone. For a moment his shoulders slumped when he realised that he was going to have to go back inside again.

It was so hard to see Abby in his home, knowing that in such a very short time she would be gone—and with her his happiness.

It was going to be just as hard to carry on working with her at St Augustine's. They'd had one night of bliss together, but how was he supposed to forget it and treat her like any other member of staff?

It might have been just one night, but it had been the culmination of months of attraction and admiration and concern and caring. For just a little while he'd thought that he had a chance that she might grow to love him too. Love would have had time to grow if she hadn't lost the baby. Nine months would have given him a chance that two days—three at the most—couldn't.

He sighed and straightened his shoulders, turning to go back for the forgotten keys. If he was lucky Abby would be so involved in her conversation with her mother that she wouldn't even notice him reach in for them.

He walked quietly into the house, and the first thing he heard was the sound of Abby crying. It was like a knife to his chest. His first instinct was to hurry to her side but he made himself pause in the hallway, just out of sight.

'No, Abby, it *wasn't* your fault. Neither getting pregnant nor losing the baby,' her mother said firmly.

'Maybe not, but marrying him *was* my fault,' Abby sobbed, tears trickling down her cheeks in a steady stream. 'He wasn't to blame for any of it and I shouldn't have made him pay like that.'

'There's nothing wrong with getting married if you love someone,' her mother pointed out in her usual logical way. 'I hear people are doing it all the time. And you *do* love him, don't you, Abby?'

Abby could no more lie to her mother now than she'd been able to as a tiny child.

'Oh, Mum, of *course* I love him,' she wailed, her handkerchief rapidly becoming sodden. 'That's why it's hurting so much to leave him. But it just wouldn't be fair to keep him tied to me when he doesn't—'

'Oh, you silly goose,' her mother interrupted with an exasperated laugh. 'Have you ever thought that...?'

A sound behind her distracted Abby from her mother's voice, and she glanced over her shoulder—straight into Ben's fiercely intent gaze. Once their eyes met she was powerless to look away, spellbound by the potent mixture of expressions she found there.

'Uh, Mum...' she said, and swallowed nervously, watching, mesmerised, as he strode towards her and took the receiver out of her hand.

'Mrs Walker?' he said swiftly. 'Ben here. I'm sorry to interrupt so rudely but, if you don't mind, I think your daughter and I have some serious talking to do.'

Abby wasn't certain what her mother said to him, but it almost sounded as if she'd laughed and wished him good luck before he put the phone down.

An electric silence stretched out between them as Abby wondered just how long Ben had been standing there. How much had he heard?

His next words told her what she didn't want to know. 'So you love me, do you?' he growled. 'You love me, and you'll tell your mother about it but you won't breathe a word of it to me!'

He was pacing furiously backwards and forwards as he spoke, and it almost seemed to Abby as if sparks were flying around the room.

'When were you going to tell me?' he demanded, suddenly coming to a halt in front of her and standing with his fists on his hips, his legs braced aggressively. 'Was it going to be before you left to go back to your flat or were you going to chicken out?'

Abby knew she'd had no intention of breathing a word to him about her feelings, afraid that he'd feel pressured to stay with her, so cowardice and guilt wouldn't let her meet his gaze.

'You idiot!' he exclaimed. 'Don't you realise how much time and energy we'd have wasted?'

The unexpected accusation finally made her look up at him, just in time to watch him crouch beside her.

'Hasn't it dawned on you yet that it was no sacrifice for me to propose to you—that I started falling in love with you the first time I met you? If you insist on making me clean up your disaster of a flat and moving you back in, I'm only going to have to pack everything up again as soon as I can seduce you into moving back here. Even without that magical night, haven't you realised that this is where you belong?'

Abby stared at him in disbelief and a single tear overflowed and trickled down her cheek.

'Well, why didn't you say so?' she demanded with a quiver in her voice, as she fought to contain the sudden explosion of joy inside her. 'I thought it was just because of the baby and—'

'That was just an excuse to do what I'd been wanting to do for weeks...months. And let me tell you, Mrs Taylor, it'll be at least a century or two before I'll willingly let you leave me.'

'That soon?' Abby teased, then squeaked in surprise when he scooped her out of her chair and onto his lap on the settee, his arms tightening possessively around her.

'Oh, Abby, I feel as if I've spent months losing you—first to my brother when he was pretending to be me, then when you accused me of attacking you.'

He shook his head and when she felt the tension in the arms holding her she was swept with new regret. If only she'd realised that there'd been two of them she'd never have made the accusation. Deep inside she'd known that he was too trustworthy a man to have been capable of such a thing.

'I'll never forget that moment in the police station when you confronted me. You looked at me with such hurt in your eyes. But that all pales when I think how close you came to dying—'

'Shh, it's all over now,' she whispered, putting her hand over his mouth to silence him and receiving a kiss for her pains. 'Your brother's well on the mend now...'

'And a completely different character since you and my mother insisted on visiting him,' Ben pointed out with a chuckle. 'I think he's a bit astounded that he's got off so lightly. As for Mum, she seems absolutely determined to "adopt" him as her long-lost son.'

'From what you've told me about his childhood, it's about time he found out what a real mother's like,' Abby said with a smile, remembering the way Mrs Taylor had welcomed her with open arms. For a woman with a badly damaged heart she was certainly overflowing with love.

Ben smiled as well, but she could tell from the sadness in his eyes that he was thinking about the baby she'd lost.

'You'll be that sort of mother too,' he said suddenly, that familiar intensity returning to his hazel eyes.

Abby basked in the compliment. She knew it was too soon yet to be contemplating pregnancy, but just the thought of the prospect warmed her to the core.

'When and how many?' she asked, suddenly realising that their lack of a normal courtship had robbed them of the chance to discuss such things before they married.

'Whenever you're ready—and a football team,' he replied quickly, then laughed at her horrified expression.

'Oh, Abby,' he said with a sigh, and tucked her securely against his side. 'Haven't you realised yet that you could ask me for the top brick off the chimney and I'd get it for you?'

'Gold-wrapped?' she challenged, with a teasing string of kisses along the edge of his jaw.

'I promise,' he replied, trapping her chin in his palm and turning her mouth to meet his. 'Delivered with a kiss.'

'And we both know that you'd do it,' she whispered against his parted lips, 'because you're such a trustworthy man.'

'Only trustworthy until your surgeon gives you the all-clear,' he warned with a wicked grin, keeping his mouth just a little too far away for her liking. 'Then the only thing you'll be able to trust me to do is make love to you until you beg for mercy.'

'Or you do…' she retaliated as she linked her fingers behind his head and pulled him down for the first of a lifetime of kisses.

Modern
romance™

...international affairs – seduction and passion guaranteed

Medical
romance™

...pulse-raising romance – heart-racing medical drama

Tender
romance™

...sparkling, emotional, feel-good romance

Sensual
romance™

...teasing, tempting, provocatively playful

Historical
romance™

...rich, vivid and passionate

Blaze™

...scorching hot sexy reads

30 new titles every month.

Live the emotion

MILLS & BOON®

Sensual romance™

...teasing, tempting, provocatively playful

4 brand-new titles each month

Available on subscription every month from the Reader Service™

Medical
romance™

...pulse-raising romance – heart-racing medical drama

6 brand-new titles each month

Available on subscription every month from the Reader Service™

...sparkling, emotional, feel-good romance

6 brand-new titles each month

Available on subscription every month from the Reader Service™

Modern
romance™

...international affairs – seduction and passion guaranteed

8 brand-new titles each month

Available on subscription every month from the Reader Service™

GEN/01/RS3